Stuart Charles Neil

THE FANTASTICAL LIGHTHOUSE

Illustrated by
Rosemary Young

The Fantastical Lighthouse

Copyright © 2018 Stuart Neil

For Leo & Maddie,
Finn and Jasmine

CHAPTER ONE

THE SCHOOL
SUMMER HOLIDAYS

When Dudley got out of bed in the morning it took him only two minutes to awaken the entire household. There were blinds on the window of his bedroom. They could be gently pulled into a roll at the top using a cord at the side, or they could be tugged downwards in the middle and whizz upwards into the roll at a hundred miles an hour. Whizz-crash! Whizz-crash! Whizz-crash! they went, making it sound as though World War Three had begun.

Yesterday had been his 8th Birthday and some of the chocolate cake from his party was still glued to the underside of his chin, making his freckled face look as if he had grown a beard overnight.

Dudley was wearing yesterday's clothes. His mother was so tired after the party that she had kissed him "Goodnight" without noticing that he had not washed, cleaned his teeth or changed into his pyjamas. Dudley thought that perhaps he should stay like this every day to save time and a lot of unnecessary washing.

All the others in the house lay awake trying to work out what had crashed with such a noise at 6.15am. Dudley wandered along the landing and barged into his sister's bedroom. Helen is 11 and is about to begin her last week at primary school. She had passed an exam to go to the Grammar School. There were only three grammar schools left in Devon and this one attracted the more clever children in the area, so her Mum and Dad were very pleased. The smile on Helen's face froze as the freckled and bearded face appeared around the bedroom door. Small brothers were all a pain and Dudley was more like being given a daily injection.

The face was grinning and, without moving its lips, said

"I am here to annoy you."

Dudley approached the bed and pulled the warm duvet off Helen and off the bed.

"Aargh - go away! I was nice and warm and dreaming of the holidays. Just one more week of school."

"I like school" said Dudley.

"Well, you can stay there. I am going to have holidays and adventures; preferably without you."

They lived in a quite a large detached house with a driveway large enough to park two cars, and set a little back from the road through the village. The back lawn reached down to a stream that was wide enough and deep enough to keep a small boat moored to a post in the bank, with a green canvas cover over it. This was to keep off the rain when the boat was not in use. Dad worked ten miles away in Exeter and was often attending meetings in Bristol or far away in London. Mum was a Dinner lady at their school in the village, so her holidays were the same as theirs. One week to go!

Dudley went downstairs and opened the back door to let out the cat.

Cats are supposed to be nocturnal animals, out at night and sleeping inside all day. But Stupid was stupid and got it the wrong way around.

You may be wondering why he is called "Stupid". When he was a kitten he lived in the house on the other side of the road with his mother, brother and sisters. He was a wanderer and explorer and, every time that Dudley's Mum saw him, he was sniffing some nice smell in the middle of the road and only just missing being squashed by passing cars. After one near miss Mum ran out and picked him up from in front of the bus, which had only just stopped in time. She took him inside, told him he was stupid and three years later he was still living with them on their side of the road.

Stupid ran down the garden to hunt mice in the riverbank. Dudley watched from the big picture window. Next weekend his cousins were coming to stay for two weeks – Polly was 9 and Andrew was 12. It was always fun with them. This time they must let him join them in their exploring adventures.

The week went slowly, very slowly, until the teachers said "goodbye" and the long summer holidays began. Helen and Dudley ran all the way home from school. Mum was already there as her dinner duties were not needed today, the school having broken up at 12 noon. No sooner had they changed out of their school uniform than a car drew up in the driveway and two more children rushed into the house and threw their arms around Helen's Mother.

"Auntie, Auntie! We've come to stay."

"I know my lovely niece and nephew. You finished school yesterday. It's good to see you again, and Maggie too"

The grown-up sisters hugged and headed for the kitchen table to talk and drink tea, whilst the children ran upstairs to find Helen and Dudley.

They ran into Helen's room and collided with Helen, who was running out to find them. Polly and Helen collapsed in a heap and all three dissolved into excited laughter. A freckled face appeared further along the landing.

"Hallo Dudley" the two visitors chorused.

"I'm coming this time" said Dudley

"Coming where?"

"With you – on the adventure. I'm big now and I'm coming".

"Well, yes, maybe. But we haven't made any plans yet" said Andrew

"What about a secret journey in the boat?" suggested Dudley

"Let's unpack and have a drink and all meet up to discuss it" said Andrew. "Meet you in Helen's room in ten minutes."

Everyone nodded and smiled.

The fun had begun!

*

Twelve-year-old Andrew was quite grown up, having just finished his second year at the big school. His birthday was in August, so he was one of the youngest in the class – a school year ahead of those born in the next month of September. This made him more confident and the two girls always treated him as a sort of leader.

"O.K." he said, after they had all had a drink downstairs. "What are we going to do for the next two weeks?"

"Boat, boat, boat" shouted Dudley, excited with his idea.

"Where would we take it?" asked Polly.

"Up the stream and down the stream" replied Dudley.

Helen said "We can only go about a hundred metres up the stream because there is a small waterfall by the Price's garden and we can't drag the heavy boat over that.".

"How far downstream does the stream join the river? asked Andrew.

"About half a mile, but there aren't any obstacles on the way"

"What would we do down there?" asked Polly, looking worried.

"Explore, explore, explore" cried Dudley.

"In the moonlight – pretending to be smugglers" added Helen

"Alright, but that would have to be late in the evening – after someone's bedtime" said Andrew, looking at Dudley.

"I'm coming, I'm coming, I'm coming" shrieked a small voice.

"Let's start in the daytime then. We can try the boat out in the daytime, perhaps for a picnic down by the river." Andrew said.

"Can we all swim?" Three voices said "Yes" together.

"How far can you swim Dudley?"

"More than five miles"

"Not that far, but he is quite good" said Helen. "He was Mrs Flynn's Flying Fish for 2016. Looks like a fish too."

"I do not!"

"Like a trout, with speckly skin"

"I don't"

"And webbed feet!"

"I do not have webbed feet. These are socks."

"We will all wear life vests anyway" said Andrew quickly.

Four excited children went to bed that night. They could hardly wait until morning for the adventure to start and were all up by 7am, dressed and waiting in the kitchen for breakfast. Andrew and Helen had laid the table and it gave Helen's Mum quite a surprise when she appeared, thinking they were all still in bed.

As soon as the meal was over they all said "goodbye" and ran down the garden. Mum knew they would all be safe with Andrew in charge and told them to be back by 1pm for lunch.

The boat was an old fibreglass rowing boat that had not been used much since their Dad had become so busy. They removed the cover

and folded it away, fixed both sets of rowlocks to hold the oars and fitted one set of oars in place. Helen found four orange lifevests in a bag and they each zipped one over their clothes.

"Everyone on board! I'll row to begin with" said Andrew

Dudley climbed over the seats into the bow and the girls sat together at the stern and fitted the heavy rudder to hang in the water, pushing the tiller for steering into the wooden socket. The stream was running quite fast as it had been raining during the week, and this helped Andrew to move downstream as Helen steered a course in the middle. They immediately went under the large weeping willow tree at the end of the garden and the branches brushed each of them in turn and nearly knocked Dudley into the water.

Andrew rowed for a while until his arms ached. Then the girls steered the boat into the bank of the stream and jumped out to see how far they had come. As they stepped on to the grass a skylark rose from the nearby field and cried a warning to other birds. The Sun was up now and warming the morning air, its rays pouring through the trees onto their faces. Andrew put on his baseball hat and Polly sang:-

"Andy's got his hat on, hip, hip, hip, hooray. Andy's got his hat on and he's coming out to play."

Dudley stayed in the boat and looked down into the still water. He didn't see the water vole watching him from only one metre away in the bank. Dudley was looking for fish. There were large and small pebbles on the bed of the stream and tufts of some sort of river weed growing amongst them. A small tree branch floated by. The stream swirled along the side, flowing through blades of grass and nettles, in and out of a deep green bush, making little whirlpools that followed each other past the stationary boat. Andrew held the boat firmly against the bank by holding on to the main stem of the green bush.

"Helen, what can you see?"

"The stream goes around a bend and then alongside a cornfield. Then all I can see is the Lighthouse on Puffin Island."

"I'll row some more and then we can stop for a drink."

They all climbed back into the boat and pushed away from the bank with an oar. Andrew rowed for another ten minutes and then handed over to Polly who, although she was only nine, was good at rowing. They stopped again and opened the big red cool box that Mum had stocked with cartons of juice and Hula Hoops and a large bag of mixed biscuits.

A heron, which had been watching them from the edge of the stream, flew across the field to find a more peaceful place to look for his breakfast.

All four children removed their sweaters in the warm sunshine and each thirstily drank a carton of cool fruit juice. The stream had widened a little so this time they decided to use both sets of oars. Polly and Helen were both rowing this time. Twice Helen missed putting one of the oars in the water and just rowed air. She overbalanced and fell on top of Polly who was sitting on the seat behind. They collapsed with laughter whilst Andrew tried to keep the boat straight with the rudder.

After a long stretch of water, the stream joined a small river. They could see Puffin Island close by – just a hundred metres beyond the place where the river joined the sea.

"Let's go to the Island" said Andrew. "The sea is calm and we have plenty of time."

"None of us has been this far before without Daddy." said Helen.

"I wouldn't let us go any further if it was windy or the river was flowing too fast" replied Andrew "and we can all swim."

They rowed out to the little island and pulled the boat up onto a tiny sandy beach between two high rocks. A path led up towards the flat centre of the island, which was dominated by a huge lighthouse that had not been used for more than 50 years.

CHAPTER TWO

TUFTY TEA

The Lighthouse on Puffin Island looked rather lonely. It was there to warn ships of the rocky headland beyond the river mouth, because on a misty day the entire headland could be hidden. Now all the ships had radar and could see the outline of the coast on screens inside their steering cabins, so the lighthouse was no longer needed.

Looking up at the red and white building the children thought it was huge. They climbed a dozen steps up to the big wooden door at the base of the building. It was closed and sealed with a hasp and the largest padlock they had ever seen. They ran down the steps again and walked around the wide base clambering over loose rocks in a couple of places.

Dudley tripped and fell on his side. There was a scurrying sound underneath him which made him stand up very quickly.

"Hey. There's a rabbit nest down here!"

"Rabbits don't have nests" said Polly. "They live down holes and burrows."

"They can't be living here – it's all rock." added Helen.

"Something scrabbled underneath me" said Dudley, certain of what he had heard.

They all gathered to investigate. 'What could it be?'

"Be careful. It may bite."

"It was down there – in the rock" Dudley pointed.

Andrew discovered that there was a straight line of grass just where Dudley had fallen, and about half a metre away two grassy lumps. When he felt through the lumps he could feel metal.

"These are door hinges" he shouted.

He quickly realized that where Dudley had landed was wood, not rock.

A ring handle was set in the wood and, if he pulled it, it came up and raised the hatch a little.

"I'll pull the handle if you three put your hands under the hatch as it rises."

This they did and the hatch easily opened and rested against the rocky side of the path. Below them were stone steps leading down into the dark.

"A secret passageway" said Helen

'Maybe used by smugglers' thought Andrew

"I don't think we had better go down without a torch" he said.

The mystery deepened when Dudley remembered that there had been a 'scrabbling' under the hatch when he first fell on it.

"Time to go home if we are going to be back in time for lunch" said Andrew. So they closed the hatch and made their way back to the little beach where the boat was sitting waiting for them.

It was harder rowing home against the flow of the stream so that when they reached the willow tree at the bottom of the garden they were quite hungry. Andrew had sent a message on his mobile that they would be half an hour late for lunch. After the meal, during which everything was eaten, the four sat on the stream bank at the end of the garden dangling their feet in the water. Everybody's thoughts were of the steps that led under the hatch and what lived down there that 'scrabbled.'

"We must go back this afternoon" said Polly, and they all agreed.

"We could take our bikes and ride along the towpath beside the stream. It would be faster" said Helen.

"But how do we get across to the Island – swim?" asked Andrew.

"No, it has to be the boat again. Helen, can you find a large torch in the house No, two? In case one runs out of battery whilst we are down in the dark."

Helen found both a large and a small torch in her Dad's garage workshop and off they went again, taking turns to row.

As they pulled into the little beach again Andrew thought 'After two weeks of this we shall be very fit or very tired'. They pulled the boat well up the beach as the tide was coming in, and tied the painter rope at the front around a piece of solid rock. Excitedly they all ran up the slope and around to Dudley's hatch.

Carefully they lifted the creaky hatch door again and rested it against the rock. Andrew switched on the larger torch and began to go down the steps.

"What if something jumps out and bites you?" asked Polly nervously

"I'll hit it with this heavy torch" replied Andrew.

They went slowly in case the scrabbling thing was waiting for them.

The steps led into a passageway that opened into a large cavern cut out of the rock. They all stood together and shone the torch around the inside of the cavern. Wondering whether it had been made by the sea or smugglers had cut it out as a secret store room, when, suddenly a booming voice said

"Hallo. My goodness you took a long time to get down here."

The voice sounded scary as it echoed in the

cavern. Startled, they all looked around, trying to see who was speaking.

"If you point the torch up here you will see me."

Andrew shone the torch around and there, sitting on what looked like a ledge, was the strangest person he had ever seen.

"You will not have seen anyone like me before. I am a Tufty and I come from another land. Come closer. Don't be scared. I won't hurt you."

They crept forward with wide eyes, looking at a person who could have been a cartoon character on the television.

"That's it. Have a good look. I may look strange to you but you look weird to me. My name is Turnip – Turnip Tufty. What are you called?"

"Andrew and Polly Harper, and Dudley Carter and I am Helen"

Turnip had a very large head for the size of his body. It was bald in the middle with tufts of hair over each ear and a tufty beard. He was only about one metre tall so his legs were tiny. He wore a yellow waistcoat with red buttons and a red and white spotted handkerchief was tied around his neck. His trousers were brown and stopped 15 cms above his shoes, which were shiny brown with large yellow laces.

"How long can you stay? I suppose you will want some Tea"

"We can stay for a while, but it is not teatime yet" Andrew answered.

"Tuftys only eat Tea and drink Tea" said Turnip. "We have Tea when we wake up, Tea in the middle of the day and Tea in the evening.

We also have Tea when anyone visits so you had better have some Tea."

"Follow me" said Turnip in such a commanding voice that the children all felt they must follow him. They also noticed that the cavern had filled with a pink light and they could see everything without using the torch. In the middle was a lake of water which looked quite deep.

All the way around it was a platform like a shelf except for the piece that must have been next to the sea, which was just rock.

"Andrew, please run back to the steps and close the hatch door."

Andrew did as he was asked and Turnip said to the others.

"I was just cleaning the inside of the hatch this morning when 'crash', something fell right on top of it. I scrabbled to my feet and ran down the steps in case it was a piece of rock that could have broken through the hatch. But then it moved and shouted and I realized that someone had passed through the 'grown-up trap' and fallen on the hatch. So I came up here and peeped through the spyhole and saw all of you discovering our secret entrance."

"What is a 'grown-up trap'" asked Helen.

"Oh. Just a piece of metal pipe that stretches 1.5 metres above the path that comes up from the beach. All the grown-ups either knock it or hold on to it as they walk past because they are taller than the pipe. Then it rings a bell in the cavern here and up in the Lighthouse as a warning that grown-ups are coming and we all need to hide." answered Turnip.

Polly said "I saw the pipe and just walked under it and so did everyone else."

"Why don't you like grown-ups?" asked Dudley

"Most of them can't see us, but those with blue eyes can. And they will go back and tell their friends we live here and in no time there will be hundreds of people all coming to look at us and eat our Tea. We like children. They can all see us and join in some of our journeys."

"You said 'us'" said Andrew. "Are there more of you living here?"

"Well, there are five Tuftys, seven Junglies, a Flummock and a Wilbur. And all the adventure boats are driven by a Trainee Superhero," said Turnip. "Now, come upstairs for Tea."

Up the stone stairs they went in single file and Turnip pressed a button in the wall to turn off the cavern lights. Through a door was another way in to the bottom of the Lighthouse. They began to climb the steps up inside the Lighthouse that went round and round, when a door in the middle opened and a tall creature came out. He had a body that was thin and long, a very worried face and hair that had not seen a comb for days, glasses on the end of his nose, no socks but enormous blue trainers on his feet. He was muttering to himself:-

"Oh Dear. 27. Oh Dear 27. It is not enough. How can I do it with only 27?" And he pushed past the children and on down the spiral stairs.

"In case you were wondering, he is the Flummock" Turnip said.

"Flummocks are always flummoxed and never know what to do. Sometimes he is so flummoxed that he forgets to make his Tea and we have to give him some of ours, or he would get even thinner."

About halfway up the stairs Polly looked out of one of the windows. They seemed to be very high up. Down below she could see their little boat on the beach and the river winding beyond, with their stream leading back past the cornfield. Wow – this was the beginning of the sort of adventure she was hoping to have in the summer holidays.

Turnip opened another door and said:-

"Come into my house." It was only one big

room, circular of course, and the square piece in the centre looked like the entrance to a lift.

"You have a lift in the Lighthouse?" asked Andrew

"Yes. It is useful when we have heavy things to carry up from the cavern, and there is an express speed for emergencies."

Dudley looked pleased. He loved lifts, especially when they went fast.

Turnip clapped his hands, and a pretty Tufty girl appeared wearing a blue dress. She had much more hair than Turnip, but it was all made of tufts that grew close together.

'This is my daughter Tania" said Turnip. "She will make us Tea."

Tania said "Hallo." and then disappeared behind the lift shaft.

A Tufty Tea was delightful. Tania Tufty brought a tray laden with scones and jam and cream. Each of the children was given a plate with two scones and told to help himself with cream and strawberry jam. Polly began to spread jam on her scone, which she had cut in half.

"No" cried Turnip. "Cream first"

"Oh. The cream is like butter that you put on first?" said Polly

"Turnip is right" answered Helen "Down here in Devon you always put cream first and then lots of jam on the top."

"If you do it the other way, the scone will not melt in your mouth" said Tania. "Now put a great big dollop of cream and lots of jam."

Strawberry jam was Dudley's favourite flavour and he managed to spoon a whole strawberry into his portion.

The scones were amazing. They were not only warm and fresh, but they slowly dissolved in your mouth without chewing. The scone feast was followed by a large mug of tea.

"I don't like drinking tea" said Dudley

"Sshhh!" said Polly. "Try to drink some or Turnip will be offended.

"But….."

"No Dudley. You must drink some. Put in lots of milk and a little sugar" said Helen.

Turnip didn't hear this because he was spooning ice cream on to a bowl of jelly. Chocolate ice cream on to orange jelly Mmmm!

"One bowl each for you to enjoy. It will taste like melted chocolate orange."

"Tell us about the boats driven by superheroes" said Andrew

"You have to book each trip. The drivers are

only Trainee Superheroes. Part of their training is to learn the magic and take other people on special journeys." answered Turnip. "They will only come when it is misty or foggy because we don't want grown-ups to interfere and spoil the fun. When the mist is around the Lighthouse no-one can see the boats come and go."

"Can we go on a trip one day?" asked Polly eagerly.

"Of course you can" said Turnip and Tania together.

The children looked at each other and Polly hugged Helen in her excitement.

CHAPTER THREE

LIVING IN THE LIGHTHOUSE

"It will cost between two and six eggs each trip, depending on where you go." said Turnip.

"Eggs!!" the children chorused.

"Eggs are more valuable than money. None of our lands have chickens and everybody loves eggs. Oh, how we love boiled eggs for Tea" Tania answered.

"I'll bring you eggs tomorrow" said Dudley. "Dozens of them if you like."

Andrew looked at Helen, who was wondering where he would find them.

"Yes please. But save some to pay for the boat trips." Turnip replied.

"Please book an adventure trip for us this week." asked Polly.

"Where would you like to go?" asked Turnip

"Scotland" said Dudley, not really knowing where it was.

"Sorry. They only go to the Cola Islands" replied Turnip

"I've never heard of the Cola Islands." said Andrew.

"But that is where everyone goes, whenever they can pay the fare.

You must come to the Outer Tufty Islands. There is Great Tufty, Middle Tufty and Tiny Tufty. We come from Great Tufty where there are Cola Falls in three flavours."

"What are Cola Falls?" Polly asked

"Waterfalls that you can drink. I wish you had them here. They are an important part of Tufty Teas on Great Tufty" said Tania.

"Cola Falls sound brilliant" said Helen, who loved fizzy drinks, especially Cola. "How many eggs will it cost to go to Great Tufty?"

"Four eggs each, return." replied Turnip. "I have a day off on Thursday. If it is misty we can go on Thursday. I will book it today."

"How long will it take?" asked Andrew. "I don't know whether Auntie will let us go if it takes too long."

"Aha" laughed Turnip. "It only takes ONE minute. There is no time for any trip with a

Superhero. The time you arrive back here will be one minute later than the time you left! It is 'Fantastical Magic'! Your Auntie will not know how far you go. But part of the magic is that you must always catch the return ferry."

Suddenly there was a 'whoosh' and the whole room shuddered. Polly grabbed hold of Andrew and Dudley covered his face with his hands.

"Turnip, what on earth was that?" asked Helen

"The express lift with all the Junglies in it. They are going down to the cavern for their daily exercise and they always press the express button on the lift."

"What will they do for exercise?" Helen asked again.

"There are lots of ropes and cables in the roof of the cavern that they have fixed to swing on and catch each other. Ever day they come down for half an hour and swing about."

"Can we watch?" they all chorused

"Yes. As long as you keep out of the way. Come back down the stairs and we will watch them from the platform at the top of the cavern."

They all scrambled out of the room and ran down the stairs and through the door. The first thing they heard was a lot of high-pitched screeches:-

"Whee, Whee, Wallup" "Yoppy, yoppy, whooo" "Aye, Aye, Aye, zoom" "Whee, wheehee"

High above the cavern lake were four or five animals or little people with long arms and legs, swinging on ropes, somersaulting and hanging onto each other. They were jumping from one rope to another or landing on one of the platforms attached to the walls. They were yelping and whooping with delight and performing like monkeys in a tree. Each one was as big as a Tufty – about one metre tall and completely green with a happy smiling green face and green arms and legs. They wore shirts and shorts or skirts that were red with black dots all over them. These made them look like large ladybirds with green legs.

The display was amazing and very clever but, when they saw one of the children, one of the Junglies forgot to catch another and he fell down into the water with an enormous splash. He rose to the surface spluttering and spitting out water and swam to the side with fast breast-strokes. He was met by two older Junglies in tracksuits, who pulled him on to the side. The children could now see that he was covered in green fur because this was dripping water on to the ledge. He was still smiling and looked to be a friendly creature. Dudley immediately decided that he loved Junglies.

"Why do they always exercise?" asked Andrew.

"They live on the only two Cola Islands that are covered in jungle – all trees and high plants and shrubs – and they have to keep fit to be able to jump from tree to tree because there are no roads and wild animals live on the ground. They only eat fruit, which grows up in the trees and so climbing, jumping and swinging are the only ways to get their Tea.

Bungle Jungle does have a harbour where the boats can dock, and it even has a short road and two shops. Mungle Jungle, however, is only forest and they have to jump from the boat and grab hold of a tree in order to get on to the land.

All the Junglies had stopped exercising and their parents were towelling down the wet one. They were watching the children and chattering and pointing. Dudley had wandered down the steps and was sitting on a step close to them. Two Junglies came up to him and touched his curly hair.

"Your fur is like ours, but it is the wrong colour."

"No," said Dudley "It's yours that is wrong. No-one has green hair"

"Well, we do. We would look silly sitting in a Mungle Jungle tree with blond or ginger hair. Where would we hide?"

"Are there lots of other creatures trying to catch you and eat you?" asked Dudley

"No. None in the trees. That is why we are always happy. The birds are singing in the trees. All the dangerous animals live on the ground and can't climb trees, so we are quite safe. We are green because we have always been green. There was one red one for a while, but only because he fell into a big pot of tomato soup during the New Years Day party."

Then Father Junglie looked at his watch and they all climbed back into the lift. The lift door closed and 'whoosh'. Up it went at a great speed.

The children heard a chorus inside of 'wheeeee"

"I must have a go in the express lift." said Dudley

"O.K." said Turnip "I'll call the lift back down". Turnip pressed the call button and the lift came slowly down to the cavern. When it stopped there was a 'sucking' noise and the doors opened. Inside, the lift was circular with 8 small seats around the wall.

"Fasten your seat belts if you want the express to work. Everybody ready?"

The doors closed and Turnip pushed the 'Express' lever. Nothing happened!

"Someone hasn't fastened his seat belt." said Turnip

It was Polly. Hers had not quite clicked into the catch. Turnip pressed again and 'whoosh'. The lift took off like a rocket and they felt as though they had left their tummies behind. There were several blurs as they passed the other floors and lift doorways, until 'boing', the lift hit something squashy that stopped it going any further upwards. The doors opened and they were looking out onto a flat platform. They stepped out carefully and found themselves on a metal floor with huge letters printed on it. Beyond the platform they could see the sea far below, and for miles along the coastline.

Andrew looked behind him and saw, above the lift shaft, an enormous thick plastic balloon that looked rather like a bouncy castle. Turnip saw him looking.

"It's only the brake that stops the express lift from going further upwards – or we could finish up in space. You are now on the helicopter platform that was built a long time ago to bring the lighthouse keepers to work and to bring their Tea whilst they looked after the light.

"Where is the light?" asked Helen

"Underneath this platform. Only one side of the light is still there. The rest of the glass room is Wilbur's home. He is too big to have one of the rooms inside the building, so he lives in the light where he can see everything going on around. But he is becoming lazy and was asleep both the times you arrived today. His job is to warn us but we think he may have to be replaced by the Cola Council. He is the only Wilbur here and rather lonely. He has read all his books, played all his computer games a hundred times and misses his family back on Rumbletum Island."

"Rumbletum Island?" exclaimed Polly.

"Yes. All the Wilburs are so hairy that they can't help eating some of their hair with their Tea. It is difficult to digest in their tummies. All over the Island there is the sound of rumbling, so you think there is a volcano about to erupt. It is only the rumbling tums of the Wilburs. The other problem on their Island is that they are all called 'Wilbur', which is extremely confusing.

"Are they scary?" asked Helen

"No, just very large and very hairy and rather rumbly. Here comes Wilbur now."

A hatch door opened in the metal floor and a large hairy arm appeared. Behind it squeezed an enormous furry creature, rather like a teddy bear with very long brown hair. He could only just get through the hatch and, when he stood up, he towered over them all. Wilbur was about three metres tall with huge brown eyes and eyelashes long enough and large enough to blow a breeze over the children every time he blinked.

"Hallo. I'm Wilbur." said a deep, friendly voice. When did you come? I must have been asleep."

"Hallo Wilbur. I'm Polly and this is my Brother and my Cousins. We found the way in by accident this morning."

"I am supposed to be in charge of this Cola Outpost." said Wilbur

"It was my prize last year for having the whitest teeth on our Island in the annual teeth-cleaning festival."

"Do you only clean your teeth once a year?" asked Dudley, suddenly very interested in this idea.

"No. Always twice every day, but the Competition is only once every year." Wilbur smiled and his teeth shone in the sunlight. "All the Wilburs have nice clean teeth and the Island dentist has sold his house and moved to another land where they drink too much cola from waterfalls. Did you bring any music?"

"No. Sorry" said Andrew. "Don't you have any here?"

"I love to dance" said Wilbur "and there isn't any music here since I trod on my CD player last week."

And with this he began to dance on the

helicopter pad. The metal shook and rattled as Wilbur twirled and danced up and down and along the centre of the platform. When he stopped there was the sound like an underground train coming trough a tunnel before it reaches the station.

Polly screamed "The platform is collapsing!"

"It's alright" said Turnip "It's only Wilbur's tummy. It always makes a good rumble after he dances"

Andrew looked at his watch.

"It's time for us to go home" he said.

"We will let you go if you promise to come back tomorrow and bring some eggs" said Turnip.

"O.K. We promise" added Helen.

"Can we go down in the express lift?" asked Dudley excitedly.

They all piled into the lift again and turned to wave to Wilbur, who smiled his lovely white smile at them before the doors closed. Then 'whoosh' – down they went. So fast that they thought they would crash through into the cavern, but the cable from the top of the lift braked their fall just at the perfect moment. Their stomachs arrived (it felt) a few seconds later.

"Do you have to row all the way home again?"

"Yes, we do" Andrew answered Turnip.

"Why not row the boat to where the river ends and tie it to one of the buoys there? Wade ashore and run along the path beside the stream," suggested Turnip. "Your boat will be safe there. Hardly anyone comes to the end of the river or to the Island and anyway, they won't take your boat. Also Wilbur will watch out, if we can keep him awake."

"Then, tomorrow we could bring our bikes and leave them by the river mouth, and only use the boat for the short journey across to you," said Helen excitedly. "It will be much quicker and easier. Andy, did Auntie Maggie bring your bikes down this time ?"

"Both of them were strapped on to the back of the car because she thought we would need them," he replied.

Down through the cavern they went and Turnip waved them off before he closed the secret hatch.

"Come soon tomorrow" he called.

The four children rowed to the bank beside the river mouth and tied the boat to a post near the bank in the shallow water. They splashed through the ankle-deep water and climbed on to the path. It was wide there and a branch ran off to one side to follow the line of the stream. They half walked and half ran along the path in single file, causing a family of swans to push off with their big webbed feet and swim out into the river and, further along the stream, coots and mallards moved away from the bank and out into the middle of the stream.

When they arrived at their garden they disturbed Stupid, who was just about to pounce on a little mouse that he had been watching for ages in the stream bank. He meowed angrily at them and ran ahead to his catflap in the back door of the house. Everybody's shoes and socks were wet from the sea water, so they took them off and left them by the back door in the evening sun.

Dudley was the first into the house:-

"Mum, Mum, we have had the best adventure ever and I was there all the time." he shouted "We saw Tufties and Junglies and there was a lift that went 'whoosh' and we are going on a fast boat on Thursday and we had cream teas and….and…."

"Yes dear. How exciting" said Mum, looking at the others and shaking her head. They looked back, shaking theirs in reply.

Helen grabbed Dudley as they reached the top of the stairs.

"We must not tell grown-ups. Remember what Turnip said?"

Dudley bit his lip and bowed his head

"I forgot" he said quietly.

They all agreed that their adventure today must be a special secret.

After an early dinner all the children went to their rooms to lie down and think about their day – the first day of the holidays – and the best start they could have imagined possible. Within twenty minutes all four were asleep. Dudley was dreaming of swinging through the trees holding a Junglie by his hand. Polly was snuggled against the fur of Wilbur's chest, which folded around her like a blanket. Helen was eating a huge scone with jam and cream, and Andrew was handing out eggs from a large basket to Junglies and Tufties, so they could all join him on the boat to the Cola Islands.

Auntie Maggie said to Mum:-

Well, that was easy. Nobody wanted to stay awake and play. I think they have all gone to sleep already. Amazing. It must be the sea air.

CHAPTER FOUR

ROCKET FERRY

The next day was Sunday and Daddy had returned home late the previous evening, after the children had fallen asleep. In the morning at breakfast he gave each of the children £1 pocket money.

"Don't spend it all on sweets" he said

Helen thought 'No. We will spend it on eggs. I was wondering how we could buy lots of eggs.

They walked down to the Farm Shop in the village and bought 6 eggs each – 24 for £4.

"Now we have enough for the ferry fare" said Helen "Let's take them today in case Turnip needs to pay the fares in advance."

Dudley was grumbling that he could have bought lots of sweets with his £1.

"You still can if you like, but you will have to

wait for your trip on a Superhero Ferry if you do" said Polly. "I'm keeping my eggs because I want to have another Tufty Tea on Great Tufty Island."

It was quite foggy this morning as they walked back home from the shop. They could hardly make out the willow tree that hung above the stream. This time Mum had made a packet of sandwiches and a carton of orange juice for each of them to take for a picnic lunch because she was going shopping with her Sister in Exeter and wanted to stay there all day.

"I expect you will eat your picnic at home and stay indoors for most of the day" said Auntie Maggie. "It is not so nice exploring in the fog."

The children looked at each other and didn't say anything. It was 9am when the four friends began to cycle along the towpath towards the Lighthouse. The mist was swirling around and was sometimes thick, meaning they could often only see as little as 10 metres ahead. Halfway along Helen was leading the single file – her box of eggs and her lunch safely in her saddle-bag – when she cycled into an especially thick patch of fog and, straight ahead, was a trailer full of hay. Before she could stop 'Thump' Helen's bike crashed into the side of the trailer! The bike stopped but Helen somersaulted over the handlebars and into the hay.

Everyone else screeched to a halt behind.

"Helen, are you O.K.?"

There was a cough and a splutter from inside the hay and Helen's head appeared through the top of the hay looking like the head of a scarecrow.

"No, I am not" she said as pieces of hay and straw fell off her head and clothes, off her ears and her face. "Who put a silly trailer right across the path?"

"Are you hurt?" asked Andrew anxiously.

"No, I don't think so" she replied picking up her bike and inspecting it for damage. "The mudguard is a little bent but everything else seems to be working properly."

But there was a yellow drip coming out of the saddlebag. Drip, drip, drip.

"Oh No! My eggs are broken" she cried, opening the saddlebag to reveal a squashy mess of eggs and shell and eggbox and a sandwich packet with a coating of egg. "Now I have no eggs to give Turnip for my fare."

"We are not going until Thursday" said Andrew. "We can find some more eggs before then"

They helped her wash the saddlebag and the packet of sandwiches in the stream and discovered that two of the eggs were unbroken.

"There, you still have half the ferry fare" said Polly.

"Let me go in front" said Andrew "I am going to cycle more slowly this time in case we find more obstacles on the pathway. The mist is very thick in places. Be careful to stay on the path or you may cycle into the stream. Helen, you go last and shout if anyone has a problem behind me."

Off they went again with Helen feeling rather shaken. The mist was not so thick at the sea edge and they could see the boat floating at the end of a short rope still tied to the tall white post. The children waded out through the water and climbed aboard. Although the Lighthouse was only 100 metres away it was hidden in the fog. Andrew worked out the direction in which they should row the boat and they quickly came to the rocks. They worked their way around to the little beach where they left the boat tied to the same rock as before.

As they walked up the steep path Andrew pulled on the 'grown-up alarm' to let Turnip know that someone was coming.

"He will watch through the spyhole and see it is only us.- if he can see far enough into the mist." said Andrew to the others.

Carefully holding their eggboxes the children reached the hatchway to find it was already open. At the bottom of the steps was Tania Tufty.

"Come quickly" she cried "or we will miss the ferry. It has been waiting for half an hour already"

"But it is not Thursday yet" said Polly.

"Come now and I will tell you what my Father has arranged" she called back.

They ran to the edge of the cavern lake where there was, moored to the side, a strange silver ship that had a cylindrical centre like the middle section of an aeroplane. It was floating on two rectangular pieces of wood that were connected to the sides of the silver centre. Windows ran all along each side and the front was shaped like a rocket. A broad-shouldered young man, wearing a tight bright blue track-suit, was jumping up and down beside the ship. Each jump was lifting him about two metres above the ground.

"Who is that?" asked Dudley "Is he a super-hero?"

"Yes, he is the superhero driver" said Tania "He's doing his fitness exercises.

The trainee superhero looked at the children through his wrap-around sunglasses and said, in a deep manly voice:-

"So you decided to turn up. Have you brought the fare? 12 eggs single or 24 eggs return. That is for 6 people.

"We don't have enough for 6 returns" said Andrew.

"That is for you all and Mr. Turnip and Miss Tania. I knew I would have problems with you humans. How many eggs do you have?"

Turnip, who was already standing on the ship, jumped on to the side and said "I took a chance that you would come with the fare and changed the booking to today when I saw there was a thick mist around the Lighthouse.

"We only have 3 boxes of 6 eggs" said Polly "Helen broke hers and there are only two good ones left"

"Well, that is 20 eggs. It means that 5 of us can go on a return trip, but one must stay behind"

"I will stay" said Tania looking rather disap-pointed.

"No. I should be the one to stay. I broke the eggs" said Helen.

"Father must go to show you around Great Tufty and you must all go because it will be your first visit to our beautiful island." said Tania.

A manly voice behind them said

"You must all go in my ship"

"You will be in trouble if your fares are short by 4 eggs" said Helen.

"If I am to be a superhero I can do anything" said the Driver "And I say that you can all come with me today"

"Thank you, thank you" said Helen "What will be your superhero name?"

"If pass all my tests and trials I will be "Zebedee Zoom", the most amazing superhero working in Africa. I will be able to read a book in 5 seconds, cook a delicious meal in 10 seconds, find drinking water for a village in 15 seconds and stop people arguing and fighting in 20 seconds.

In 25 seconds I will find enough food for a whole country and in 30 seconds I will be able to Zebedee Zoom back to my home in the Cola Islands."

"All Aboard! All Aboard! This ferry leaves in two minutes!"

Everyone scurried aboard and took a seat facing forward, towards the front where Zebedee Zoom climbed into a padded chair in the pointed nose of the ferry. There were 8 seats on each side – just like a small plane, with seatbelts on each seat. The children immediately put on the seatbelts. Four of the seats were already occupied by young Tufties, whom the children had never seen before.

"Where have you come from?" asked Polly

"From France" they replied. "It's misty there today too."

"Stand by" said Zebedee. "Doors are sealed. O-be-doe Here we go"

He pushed a lever forward and the ship slowly moved away from the edge, across the lake and out through two enormous doors in the rockface that the children had not noticed before. They must have been open all the time this morning.

Andrew looked back from the ferry and saw the door in the rockface slowly closing. The mist had thinned enough for him to just see a big hairy arm waving from the helicopter platform at the top of the Lighthouse.

"Wilbur is awake and waving 'goodbye' to us. He must have been asked to close the rock doors." said Andrew.

As he was speaking everyone felt a sudden pull. The ship's engine noise increased and they started to go forward faster. Zebedee was pushing forward a different lever and the ship began to lift upwards with only the wooden skis skimming over the water, leaving a spray of sea water behind. Now he was pushing and pulling other levers, one on each side of his chair and, from underneath where they were sitting, a wing opened out on each side. The children could hardly believe that the ship was turning into a plane.

Faster they went and the ferry skis lifted off the water and rose into the air. This time Zebedee Zoom was pulling backwards on the steering wheel in front of him. Dudley looked out of the window to see one of the wooden skis folding into the place where the wing had been. This was very special. Helen had been in a plane. `Andrew and Polly too, but it was the first time for Dudley.

Up and up they went, high into the blue sky, above the layer of mist and fog that they left far below. Zebedee levelled the plane and increased the speed by pushing the lever to the word 'fast' on the frame. The powerful engine noise settled back to one with which they could speak and be heard by the person sitting in the next seat.

Zebedee took down a microphone from a hook above his head and began to speak:-

"Good Morning, passengers. This ferry is heading straight to Great Tufty in the Cola Islands. We will land on the water in 10 minutes, so please keep your seatbelts fastened. In a moment our speed will increase to 'superfast' – the flying speed of all superheroes – so do not be frightened." He pushed the lever beyond the word 'fast' to 'superfast' and the engine went 'BOOM' making the plane go ten times faster. All the clouds and the blue sky became just a blur. The children closed their eyes for it all seemed too exciting to be true.

"Tea is available on your flight" the pilot/driver continued. "Just press the button marked 'Tea' on the back of the seat in front of you and you will be served instantly."

Helen was quite hungry after her tumble into the hay trailer and all the cycling. She pressed 'Tea' and a small table immediately folded down from the back of the seat in front. A little door slid open behind it and steam came out of the space that had appeared in the chair back. Behind the steam came a plastic cup of tea and a plate with a large scone sitting on it that already had jam and cream on the top. The jam was blackcurrant on this scone – Helen's favourite flavour. She took a bite from the scone, which deliciously melted in her mouth leaving a taste of creamy blackcurrant. She shared her cup of tea with Polly, who was thirsty after her cycle ride.

"Do you think our bikes will be safe beside the sea?" asked Polly

Andrew answered "Yes, we put the cycle locks around the signpost so I think they will still be there when we return. Remember, this whole trip is only going to take one minute."

Helen finished her scone and drank the last mouthful of tea. As she pushed the empty plate and cup into the seat back and folded up the tray, she was sure a small voice said 'thank you'.

"It seemed to come from the tray" she said to Polly.

Zebedee Zoom was now reducing their speed and pulling and pushing levers and his small steering wheel. Small clouds came into view as their speed dropped and then the wooden skis came back out from under the plane and clicked into the places they had been before.

The plane landed smoothly on the calm water beside an island with sandy beaches and green trees and fields. The wings folded back into the plane as they moved slowly towards a little harbour, passing a boat with three small people pulling in a fishing net. One of them waved to the ferry whilst the others continued pulling in the heavy net.

The ferry moved through the harbour entrance and moored beside a stone jetty. Lots of Tufty people were clapping and waving. Two of them took the ferry's ropes and tied them to thick posts on the jetty.

Zebedee pushed the final lever and switched off the engine. He turned to the passengers and said:-

"Here we are at Great Tufty. I hope you enjoyed the ride."

Then he opened the door and stepped out to a cheer and several young Tufties chorusing 'Zebedee Zoom, Zebedee Zoom, Zebedee Zoom'.

He put his sunglasses back on and smacked his fist against his chest in a superhero acknowledgment.

The young Tufties from France then came off the ferry. A group of friends pushed their way through the crowd to greet them. There were hugs and some tears of joy:-

"Bonjour, bonjour mes amis, mon fils…." they cried "Allo, allo ma belle soeur. Venez ici. Venez ici"

Then came Turnip and Tania to be greeted by Turnip's wife.

"Oh how I have missed you both," she said "but this time I can come back with you."

Last came the four children. All the chatter stopped and everyone stared.

Then they began smiling and someone clapped her hands. In a moment everyone was clapping and shouting 'Welcome to the Tufty Isles' 'Come and stay with us' 'Look – we have four new visitors to Tuftytown' 'Did you bring any eggs ?"

CHAPTER FIVE

GREAT TUFTY

The rocket ferry had come to Tuftytown, the biggest town in the Outer Tufty Isles. All the house were painted in bright colours and the shops on the main street had white awnings or white painted front walls with the names of the things they had for sale printed in large letters.

Andrew thought this was better than the shops he knew, which only had the name of the owner on the front and not what was being sold. As he looked along the street he could see signs saying 'Baker' 'Fish' 'Vegetables' 'Bicycles' 'Tins of Food' 'Ladies Clothes'.

There were not many cars but strangely they all seemed to be the same make. Turnip told him they were 'Carrot Cars' and all made in a factory on Tiny Tufty. Many of the people living there worked in the 'Carrot Factory'.

"There's an orange one" said Dudley, pointing. Is it made out of carrots?"

"Ha ha ha No" said Turnip "Cornelius Carrot was the man who designed the car and started the factory to make them. The business still uses his name. I don't think cars made out of carrots would last very long on the island because we have lots of donkeys and ponies and they would eat them.

Andrew said "All the cars are the same at the front, but the back is sometimes different"

"Yes. You are quite correct" replied Turnip "Everybody who can afford to buy a car buys the front part with the engine in it and two seats for the driver and passenger to sit beside him. Then they can buy and slot on to the back another section, which has the back wheels on it. This back section can have two more seats, or it can be open with a flat area to carry things on. If you want a longer car you can slot on a section with another two seats, or another flat piece and turn it into a lorry. This makes it easy for garages to repair any broken cars because they are all the same and the mechanics only have to learn about one type of engine and one type of car body."

"They are all bright colours too" said Polly

"I like them better than our cars, which are mostly black or silver."

"We can tell how old they are by their colours" said Tania "Last year the colour was light blue, the year before was yellow. This year all the new cars are pink, so lots of ladies are trying to buy cars this year. Look, there is a brown one – that was made over ten years ago."

"Mr. Carrot is a clever man" said Helen

"Cornelius Carrot went to heaven a long time ago" said Turnip "Now the factory is owned by his grandson, Charlie Carrot. I have heard that Charlie has designed a more powerful engine for the new cars next year.

We shall all have a ride in a carrot car later today."

Turnip's wife was plump and cheerful.

"You must come along to our house now – for Tea" she said "My name is Mathilda, but everyone calls me Tilly"

So they followed Turnip, Tilly and Tania along the main street of Tuftytown, past a shop with the sign 'Cakes' above it, and a scrumptious selection of cakes and buns, of chocolate sweets and pastries and large birthday cakes in the window.

"Come on Dudley, or you will lose us" said Polly, pulling on his arm as he studied a large iced doughnut through the glass of the window.

At the top of the street was a row of houses in blue, yellow and white colours – some with different coloured chimneys. The Tufties turned into this row. Helen and Andrew, walking together, waited for a light blue Carrot Car to pass by and then followed them.

"The driver bought that car last year" said Andrew "Light blue was last year's colour."

After Tea (at lunchtime) Tilly said that she and Tania must pack a suitcase so that she could come back on the ferry. Turnip went into the yellow garage beside the little yellow house. The children had to duck their heads under each doorway because Tufties are quite short, so the ceilings and doorways are lower than in human houses. They came outside to find Turnip slotting an extra section on to the back of a red car.

"Now there will be a seat for each of us" he said "My car is four years old. I bought it in the 'red' year. Climb in and we shall go for a drive around the island."

Everybody eagerly climbed into a car seat and clicked his seat belt.

They drove back down the main street of Tuftytown and out along the coast road. Turnip seemed to wave to someone he knew every minute of the ride. There were not many cars on the road, but there were several ponies towing little trailers that he called 'traps' with one or two tufties sitting in them.

"Most people living outside the towns cannot afford to buy a car, so they ride around in a 'pony and trap'" said Turnip.

In the fields were cows and pigs and a few sheep, all happily eating grass or food left in troughs by the farmers.

"Why are there no chickens?' asked Helen.

"Five years ago they all caught 'Cola Comb'. This is a nasty disease which only affects hens. It makes the little red comb on the top of their heads shrivel up and they stop laying eggs and sometimes die. We have brought more hens from your country, but they all seem to catch 'Cola Comb'. Now we have no hens and no eggs."

"Is there no cure?" asked Andrew.

"Not for 'Cola Comb', but the vets think it could be stopped if we turn off all the cola waterfalls. They think there is always some cola in the air because of these. It only seems to affect chickens. The Cola Council has decided that we must keep them turned on because we send the cola to so many countries for them to put into bottles and cans. Because of this we now have to bring all our eggs from abroad, which is quite difficult and expensive." Turnip looked quite sad. "I like chickens. We used to keep some in our garden and could always have eggs for Tea"

The car turned towards the centre of Great Tufty island and there, rising high above everything else, was a tall mountain shaped very much like an enormous ice cream cone. It grew out of the ground and was grassy up to about

50 metres. Above that there was bare light brown rock that looked like a cone. Next, above the cone, was white snow that went up with a rounded top, just like ice cream on the top of the cone.

"It is definitely an ice cream" said Polly as they drove closer "Mmm, the largest one I have ever seen."

"You can't eat our mountain" said Turnip with a smile "because that is where all the cola comes from. Can you see a waterfall now?"

Near the base of the cone was what looked like a brown waterfall. They drove nearer and parked close by. A line of Carrot Cars, with trailer sections attached to each one, was waiting its turn to reverse close to the falls. A large tube was held under one part of the falling cola and the liquid flowed into a square tank on each trailer – one at a time. When full the driver passed the tube to the next car and drove off.

"This is the caramel flavoured fall" said Turnip "These cars or lorries are taking the cola to the shops in the towns and some to ships, which will sail abroad to deliver to lands like yours. There are two more falls like this at different places around the mountain – one with Cherry Cola and the other with Butterscotch Cola."

"I think I shall ask Mummy to move so that we can live here" said Helen.

"Do you only eat Tea with cakes, ice cream and scones and cola?"

Andrew asked Turnip.

"No, no" he answered. "If we did, it would not be long before all our teeth fell out. Every morning Breakfast Tea has cheese from the cows' milk and brown bread from the baker, and an egg if we are rich enough to be able to buy one. And Evening Tea is usually called Vegetable Tea. We have delicious soup made from four different vegetables and lots of fruit – apples and plums and raspberries from Middle Tufty, and bananas and oranges from Mungle Jungle."

"Cheese for breakfast!" said Dudley "I wouldn't like that, and Mum says that brown bread is good for me, but I don't like that either."

Andrew told him that many people in countries in Europe have cheese for breakfast, although he had never seen anyone eating it for breakfast in England.

A girl was sitting beside the waterfall filling small cups with cola and handing one to anybody who was thirsty. Helen had to try some:-

"It is delicious. The same as you had in your house Turnip"

"They are both caramel cola. My own favourite is the new butterscotch flavour. Back in the car everyone. We must move on or we shall miss the ferry back to the Lighthouse."

On they went, past a place which cares for donkeys that had been badly treated when they lived in other countries, through several villages and past a smaller lighthouse that Turnip said was still working.

A different ferry had just landed on the water – its skis sending up two plumes of sea water. They were almost back at Tuftytown Harbour.

Quickly Turnip drove to his house and parked his car in his yellow garage. Tilly and Tania were waiting with their bags packed and two precious eggs for Tilly's fare. They all walked together down the main street to the harbour. The same ferry was still moored to the jetty wall and there were now two others alongside it. One had come from Tiny Tufty and most of the people arriving had ginger tufty hair. Turnip and Tilly waved to one family they knew.

Standing beside the Lighthouse ferry was Zebedee Zoom, talking to one of the other trainee superhero drivers. He was shorter and more muscular than Zebedee and wore a helmet that was round at the front and pointed at the back.

"Shaped for speed like the racing cyclists wear" said Andrew

He also had a large T on his chest (for Trainee) and the same wrap around sunglasses as Zebedee. His skintight suit was all red and his shorts were yellow.

"Welcome back" said Zebedee. "Meet my friend, who has come over from Tiny Tufty today and will soon be going to Ireland with new passengers. He is going to be a superhero called 'Rupert Rocket'.

"Hello" said Rupert in another deep, manly voice. The children replied and Polly wished she had brought her camera to take a photo and show all her friends at school.

"We are just waiting for a Junglie who arrived on a ferry from Mungle Jungle. He has just gone in to town to buy potatoes to take to his friends in the Lighthouse." said Zebedee.

"Potatoes as presents. Poo!" said Dudley

"Don't be rude Dudley" said his big sister. "Remember they live high in the trees and will hardly ever have potatoes which grow in the ground. It will be a treat for them."

"Only if they turn them into chips" muttered Dudley to himself.

The Junglie arrived back and greeted each child by shaking hands with his green, curly-haired paw.

"All Aboard" called Zebedee, taking egg fares from Tilly and the Junglie. And off they went again in the ferry-plane; first slowly until outside Tuftytown Harbour, and then faster up on the skis, then the wings folded out and the plane lifted off the water with the skis clicking into place under the passenger area. Zebedee flew once around the Island so that the children could see it from the air. The Cola Ice Cream

Mountain looked wonderful in the centre, and they could see the two other cola waterfalls. Then 'Boom' as their clever pilot pushed the controls to 'superfast'.

"Zebedee Zoom went Boom" said Dudley to himself. A few minutes later, and after another scone and tea from the seat backs, they found themselves landing on the water again in a thick mist. The ferry motored up to the rockface where the doors were sliding open. They were back on the Lighthouse Lake and climbing out of the ferry/plane and waving thanks to their own trainee superhero.

There were three Junglies waiting to catch the ferry, all with their eggboxes held carefully. Zebedee put their bags on board and the ferry moved slowly out through the rock doorway.

"It's good to be back at the Lighthouse with you all" said Tilly.

"We must go home now" said Andrew "We are all tired and Polly went to sleep on the ferry plane. Thank you so much Turnip for a wonderful adventure."

"Can we go again?" Polly and Dudley both asked at the same time.

"Yes, of course. When it is misty – and don't forget the egg fares.

Bye!" cried Turnip.

The children wearily climbed the stone steps under the hatch and opened it into the misty air. They found the boat where they had left it and rowed back towards the land. It was difficult to find the spot where they had padlocked their bikes because the mist was still swirling in thick and thin patches. Andrew decided to climb out when the boat first hit the land and then to pull the boat along beside the towpath until they reached their bikes. Helen also climbed out of the boat to help pull it along.

"It can't be much further" she said.

"I think we may be going the wrong way" said Andrew. So they turned around and pulled the little boat with its two passengers back to where they had started. No sooner had they begun to walk in the mist the other way than they saw the signboard with their bikes resting against it.

"Oh. It was only a few metres from where we landed" groaned Helen. "I'm exhausted."

They sat down and ate their sandwiches and the drinks that had all been left in the saddlebags of their bicycles. Whilst sitting there the mist began to break up. A light breeze blew it slowly away to allow the rays from the Sun to warm them. The path was clear now and they cycled towards their village and the bottom of the garden, carefully going around Helen's haycart. Stupid was waiting for them, lying in a patch of sunlight. He greeted them with a 'miaow' before continuing to lick his paws clean. Andrew put his bike away in the garage and the others followed, stacking theirs against Andrew's and leaving space for the car when it returned.

Mum and Auntie Maggie were sitting at the kitchen table talking.

They had decided not to go shopping in the fog and were surprised that the children had gone out.

"I am not surprised you came back quickly" said Mum

"But we have been.......ow!" Poor Dudley had received a sharp kick on his ankle.

"The mist is very thick along the river" said Andrew quickly. "And rather cold. We'll stay indoors for a while and go out again later."

The children ran up to Helen's bedroom and Andrew looked at the clock on her bedroom wall.

"It is only eleven o'clock in the morning" he said "Of course, of course – our adventure only took ONE MINUTE! And the journey to and from the Lighthouse just over an hour. We had better try to stay awake or the grown-ups will be suspicious and ask a lot of questions."

CHAPTER SIX

A SURPRISE JOURNEY

None of the children was hungry when lunch-time came because they had eaten breakfast, tufty tea, ferry scones and also their packed lunch, all before eleven am.

"Mummy will wonder why we are all so tired in the middle of the day" said Helen. "We must go back out of the house and away somewhere so she doesn't notice."

"It is so warm in the lovely sunshine. Perhaps we could sleep at the bottom of the garden near the willow tree" said Polly rubbing her eyes.

"I have a better idea. Was the hay in the trailer you crashed into wet or dry, Helen?" asked Andrew.

"Quite dry, but rather pokey" she replied.

Andrew continued "There are two old

blankets in a cupboard in the garden shed. Lets take them and go back to the trailer. We could lie on the hay in the trailer and sleep for an hour without anyone knowing. If we take our bikes the grown-ups will not notice it is different to any other afternoon."

They all went downstairs and called 'goodbye' to Mum and Aunt, collected the bikes again and the two blankets, and slowly cycled beside the stream towards the sea.

"I have a feeling something has changed with the children" Auntie Maggie said.

Mum replied from the sitting room, where she was dusting a bookcase

"They seem fine to me – not just running everywhere as they usually do. Polly did look rather tired for eleven o'clock in the morning."

"You don't think they have been staying up half the night talking and playing, do you?"

"No. We would have heard them. I looked into their rooms once last night and they all seemed to be fast asleep."

"Perhaps I am imagining it" said Maggie.

Four bicycles stopped beside the trailer full of hay. No-one was to be seen in any direction, except for a small plane flying in the distance.

They put the bikes under the farm trailer and

climbed on to the hay, making a dip so they would not be seen by passers-by. Helen laid the blankets on top of the hay so they could lie down without the stalks poking into their arms and legs. Polly and Dudley went to sleep as soon as they lay on the blankets. Helen lay on her back and looked up into the blue sky.

"I hope it will be misty again tomorrow" she said to Andrew. "We shall have to wait and see. I am still thinking our adventure this morning was like a dream. Were we really awake and meeting Tufties and Superheroes?"

"We all had the same dream, so it must have been real" replied Andrew.

Helen shielded her eyes from the Sun and just looked at the blue sky

"If you lie like this without moving you can see little transparent shapes twisting and twirling in the air. They are like little creatures or transparent fairies playing in the sunshine"

She looked at Andrew, who was already asleep, and then went back to watching her fairies.

*

They didn't hear the engine of the farm tractor as it drove across the field next to them. All four were dreaming of brightly coloured cars and cups of caramel cola. Suddenly, beneath them, there was a loud 'clunk' and the whole trailer moved a little. Andrew woke up with a start, wondering where he was. Then he quickly remembered and looked over the top of the hay to see two men climbing up into the tractor. The tractor roared its engine and began towing the trailer full of hay and children across the field.

By now all the children were wide awake and looking at the tractor. Both men were not even glancing back to see if anything was wrong. Helen looked back to where the trailer had been – across the towpath by the stream. The farmer's men had not noticed their bicycles hidden underneath and had pulled the trailer away, leaving four bikes lying on the ground by the towpath. The noise of the tractor was deafening, so Helen had to shout for Andrew to hear.

"What shall we do?"

The field was uneven and the trailer was bouncing as it moved along.

Dudley and Polly were being rolled in the hay and becoming mixed up with the blankets. Andrew and Helen held on to one of the hay bales that had been placed against the sides of the trailer to hold loose hay in the centre. Andrew was thinking, and then said

"If the tractor stops at the field gate we can jump off the back."

But the gate from the first field was open and they drove straight through. By this time Polly and Dudley had managed to crawl and lean on the same bale as the others. They were both covered in pieces of hay and looked like two moving scarecrows. Now the tractor was driving them along the side of a field growing yellow rape seed. The bright yellow flowers had a strong smell.

"The smell is worse than those old blankets that we were lying on" said Polly.

They could all now see into the next field where a herd of black and white cows were grazing on thick grass. One of the men jumped down and ran ahead to open the gate. The driver kept on going right through the open gate and into the field full of cows.

"Quick, hide in the hay" said Andrew

The children dived back into the loose hay in the middle of the trailer. Andrew had realized that, as they passed through the gate, the driver's assistant would be standing there waiting to close it behind them. He would see the children. They all stayed completely still until – disaster – just as the gateman ran past them towards the tractor, Dudley sneezed loudly! Each child held his/her breath waiting for the shout as they were discovered.

"Bless you Bill" the man called. The tractor engine was still going, but quietly because it had stopped for him to catch up. The farmer, who was driving, had not heard the sneeze above the noise of the engine. He looked rather puzzled.

"Bless you too, George, on this lovely sunny day."

This was a piece of luck that made the children relax as they poked their heads out again and they could all breathe easily. George thought it was the farmer driver who had sneezed. The dented old trailer continued across a very wide area of grass as the cows stepped aside for it to pass.

The four held on tightly. On the far side was

a country lane that they were bumping towards, and getting closer to a big double five-barred metal gate. This time a lady walking her dog on a lead along the lane saw them approaching. She undid the catch on the gate and opened both parts for the tractor.

"Thank you, Mrs Parsons" called the farmer

"Oh No! We are not going to stop for this gate either" said Helen.

The tractor passed through and almost stopped because the turn into the narrow lane was very tight. The trailer was only just beginning to go through the gateway. Andrew saw that they were on the right hand side and the tractor had turned to the left. Mrs Parsons was holding the gate on the left side as well.

"Quick, jump – everyone jump."

They all landed on the grass and Polly fell forward in a somersault. But Dudley was unlucky. He landed 'Squelch' in the middle of a huge cowpat. They ran along the side of the field beside the hedge and were almost 50 metres away before the first grown-up saw them. It was Mrs. Parsons.

"Hey, come back. You are not allowed in this field" she cried.

They carried on running as fast as their legs would go.

"Mr Dodds. Did you know there were children on your trailer?"

The tractor stopped and the farmer called back

"We didn't see anyone. I think you must be mistaken. They were probably hiding by the hedge here. How many did you see?"

"3 or 4. Or it may have been 6 or 7. My eyesight is not so good these days" replied Mrs Parsons.

"Well I hope they close any field gates properly. Can't have my animals roaming about the village. Thanks for opening the gate for us,

How is your Michael's arthritis these days?"

When they saw that they were not being followed the children sat on the grass and slowly caught their breath.

"You sound like a dog panting" Dudley said to Polly.

"Well you smell like our Labrador after she has been rolling in cow poo. Keep away from me. Pooh, what a pong!"

Poor Dudley had poo all over his trainers and his socks, and some on his freckled legs. They stood up again and began to walk across the grassy field, watching out for more brown mountains left by the cows. Polly noticed that most of the cows were looking at them and two, which had been lying down, stood up and started to walk towards her. She whispered to Helen

"I think they are following us and they are very big"

"They are big, but quite harmless" replied Helen, who had always lived in the country and near fields and meadows full of cows. "They are probably wondering why we are walking across THEIR field and want to have a closer look. Don't be frightened. Look at their lovely black and white skin. Touch it. It is like short fur and the skin on their faces is like velvet."

"What if one of them is a bull and is angry that we are in his field?"

"The bull will be in another part of the farm and not with the cows when they are grazing grass to make milk."

A big Friesian went up to Dudley and pushed her wet nose and thick lips against him.

"She thinks you are another cow because you smell like her" said Polly, who started laughing at her own joke.

"Keep walking" said Andrew "Or the whole herd will be arriving to sniff and investigate us. We need to get back to our bikes."

They walked to the field gate and closed it carefully behind them, leaving four cows leaning on the top of the gate saying 'goodbye' with their beautiful eyes and long eyelashes. Then they walked alongside the yellow field of rape, keeping away from Dudley, who was behind them and looking rather sad. Soon they reached the bicycles lying by the towpath near the stream.

Andrew picked up his red bike and looked at the others. There were bits of hay and straw stuck to their clothes, in their hair and clinging to their socks and shoes. He pulled two stalks from under his hat and noticed pieces over

Polly's ear and several stalks in the neck of Helen's shirt.

"Let's pick the hay from each other before we go home" he said.

"You can do Dudley" said Polly to Andrew.

"We will all do Dudley" Andrew replied. "Dudley. Sit down beside the stream with your legs and feet in the water"

They chose a shallow part of the stream and tore handfuls of grass from the bank to rub all the cow poo from his legs and most from his socks and trainers.

"How can we explain Dudley's wet and pooey clothes to Mum when we get home?" asked Polly

"Easy" said Helen "We can tell her the whole of this adventure. Only the Lighthouse needs to be kept a secret from grown-ups".

Of course, all the trailer tale can be told. They all cycled home smiling and laughing, wet and still a little pooey.

CHAPTER SEVEN

THE EGG HUNT

"Where on earth have you been to get so wet and smelly and covered in straw?" asked Auntie Maggie as she met Dudley in the doorway of the house. She helped to put all the children's clothes into the washing machine whilst they stood watching, wrapped only in towels.

They told her the story of the hay trailer and the surprise journey across the fields, the large friendly cows and Dudley jumping into the biggest cowpat in the field.

"I couldn't help it" cried Dudley "The cow had left it in the wrong place". Everyone laughed.

The girls showered first followed by the two boys. After Mum and Auntie had said 'goodnight' the girls crept into the boys' bed-room and they all sat on Andrew's bed.

"What shall we do tomorrow?" said Polly.

"Back to the Lighthouse" added Dudley

"We need to take lots of eggs for presents and for ferry fares on the rocket ships" said Helen.

"Let's think how we can get eggs before we fall asleep tonight" said Andrew "and then hope for another misty morning."

They all lay in their beds thinking before, one by one, they fell asleep.

The next morning Helen awoke and went

straight to the bedroom window to look out across the garden, hoping for mist or fog. There was a glow in the East as the Sun, which looked as if it had had an early breakfast, smiled brightly on all the countryside. Helen was usually delighted when the sun was shining. However, today, it meant that a ferry rocket ship would not be able to come into the secret Lighthouse harbour without being seen by lots of grown-ups.

"We shall have to stay in the Lighthouse, or find something to do nearer home" she said to Polly, who was stretching in the bed opposite as she woke up from a deep sleep and dreams of Tufties and Wilburs and large velvety cows with long eyelashes.

They all washed and dressed in clean clothes after yesterday afternoon's experience. Then, after breakfast of fried eggs on toast and pine-apple juice and a croissant with butter, they all sat in a row at the bottom of the garden to plan the day. Stupid was looking into the stream where he had seen two small trout swimming past a few moments ago.

Andrew began the planning for the new day's adventures

"First, we must fetch the boat and bring it

nearer home in case someone decides to borrow it"

"Or steal it" added Dudley

"Yes, that would be a shame, and Daddy would not be very pleased when he found out" said Helen.

"We could use it to visit the Lighthouse today, but we really need to find eggs to thank our new friends and be ready with the fares for any more ferry trips." Andrew went on to say "Lets fetch the boat and then go on an egg hunt."

"Daddy planned an Easter Egg Hunt for us in the garden this year" said Dudley. "Mine was tied to a branch up in the beech tree."

"We don't need Easter Eggs, Dudley" they all replied.

They talked for a long time about ways to gather eggs and finally decided that the only way was to earn some money and buy them in the farm shop down the road.

"I could catch fish and sell them." said Dudley, who had not yet even seen a fish on this school holiday.

The girls thought they could put on a show of dancing and a short play. They would invite people in the village to pay to see it. Andrew said he would do errands for people on his bike. The problem was that some of these ideas would take a lot of time and use up all the holiday.

"Your idea sounds the best Andrew" said Helen.

They decided that they should go around the village in pairs and knock on doors to ask if they could do any jobs for the grown-ups in the houses.

They would ask for £1 for every job they did and say the money would go towards buying eggs for people who did not have any, and towards a boat trip for people, who did not have the fare. This, of course, was quite true.

Mummy and Auntie Maggie agreed that they could do this, provided they only visited people they knew and finished the jobs before dark.

"Isn't it nice that our children are going to spend their holiday helping others" said Mum.

"And use the money to help poor people. Strange though that the money is going to people without eggs. Why not 'bread' or 'milk' or just 'food'." Said Auntie Maggie.

"I don't know' answered Mum. "My children do odd things these days but, as long as they are safe and happy, Ray and I are happy too."

The four friends cycled off to fetch the boat from its mooring. They found it with two herring gulls standing as guards on the bow.

"Thank you, birds. Now we have to take our boat home"

First Andrew, and then Polly and Helen together, and then Andrew again rowed the boat along the side of the river, into the stream and then all the way home. They showed Dudley how to sit in the stern and steer a straight course with the rudder. He was quite good at it by the time they reached the willow tree.

After a glass of milk and two biscuits each Helen and Polly walked along the road to the end of the village, which was only 200 metres away.

Dudley and Andrew cycled along and began to knock on the house door at the other end of the pretty village street. The door was opened by Mrs Clark, whose daughter was in Dudley's class at school. She was pleased to see them and asked them to pull out the weeds from her husband's vegetable patch in the back garden because he had hurt his back and had difficulty bending down to do it himself. When they had finished weeding around all the carrots and lettuces and beetroot, she gave them £1 each.

"I think the eggs were costing £1 for 6" said Dudley as they pushed their bikes to the next person they knew. "That means we can buy 12 eggs already."

"Yes" replied Andrew "You can have 'A star' for maths."

"Good morning, boys. What can I do for you?" asked Derek Brown, who had taken a day off from his building business.

"Do you have any jobs that we can do for £1?"

"Yes I certainly have" he answered. "When I

was a Boy Scout we did the same as you. It was called 'bob-a-job' then. A 'bob' was a shilling – the same as 5p today. Now I see that the price is £1. I suppose everything costs a lot more now."

A lorry had dumped a pile of bricks on Mr. Brown's driveway. The boys had to stack them neatly beside his garage. They were tired when they finished and each received £2 and a big glass of blackcurrant squash.

"24 more eggs" said Dudley with a smile.

Meanwhile, the girls had arrived at the Vicarage and had spoken to Dorothy, who was cleaning the house whilst the vicar and his family had gone away for a week's holiday.

"You can help me clean and polish all these ornaments if you like and I will pay you." said Dorothy.

So they dusted and cleaned lots of large and small ornaments whilst Dorothy polished the brass and silver ones. They worked for an hour.

Dorothy said that the vicar paid her £8 per hour to do the cleaning and she would give half to the girls. So they had £4 to share.

"Wow, that will buy 16 eggs" said Polly

"More than that" corrected Helen "£1 will buy 6 eggs, so £4 will buy 24"

"That is brilliant" said Polly "I am not very good at maths"

They walked onto Mrs Walker's cottage, who asked them to go down to the shop in the village and buy some groceries for her. They were heavy things that she found difficult to carry all the way back to her house. Helen and Polly bought potatoes and milk, washing powder and several tins. They also bought stamps and posted a parcel for Mrs Walker in the Post Office section of the shop.

"Thank you very much, my dears. You have saved my old legs from walking a long way. Please come again. Here is your £1 each."

By now it was lunchtime and all four children headed home hungry. They were very happy sitting at the lunch table.

"We did 2 hours work and were paid £6" said Polly. "I'll bet that was more than you had in your 2 hours, ha,ha."

"It is not" shouted Dudley "We each earnt £3, making £6 too. Na-na nana-na!"

"That's enough" said Mum "You have all worked and done very well for one morning. And you collected our boat."

Into the room came Dad

"Hallo, everyone. Am I too late for lunch?"

He kissed Mum and was greeted by Auntie

Maggie and all the children with cries of 'Daddy, Daddy' and 'Hallo Ray' and 'Uncle Ray, you're home' all at the same time.

"I drove back from Plymouth today with Jeremy Kerslake, who lives in that big white house near the river. He told me that he had been looking out of his office window and had seen my boat, the 'Huckleberry Finn", with four children in it rowing across to Puffin Island."

The children went quiet and looked down at their empty plates on the table. They were expecting to be grounded for days. But Dad went on:-

"He said that there was some very good rowing and steering, and he knew it was not easy to steer a boat into the narrow beach between the rocks. Now Mr. Kerslake sails a nice yacht with a cabin and it is moored in the river near his house. He has a tender – a little rowing boat – that he pulls up the slipway that runs from the bottom of his garden to the river. When he realised that you were rowing all the way down the stream, then down a short piece of the river and then across to the Island, he kindly said that you could leave Huckleberry Finn on his slipway. He thought you may want to explore the river during the holidays. And you can leave your bikes when you are in the boat."

"Thanks" said Andrew. "That will save a lot of time and hard rowing"

"I am quite happy for you to use our boat provided you are very careful over safety. You must always wear your lifejackets"

"We do" all four chorused.

"Mr. Kerslake said that he was watching you once through his telescope and one of the girls did not have a lifevest!"

"It was not us" said Helen

"Yes, it was" said Polly quietly. "It was me. You didn't see because we were rowing together and you sit in front of me. It is difficult to row with the padded lifejacket on, so I took it off just for rowing."

"Promise you will not do it again, Polly" said Dad.

"I promise, Uncle Ray. I know if the boat capsized I would need it to help me float."

"Good girl. Now, what were you going to the Island for? It is only a pile of rocks and the Lighthouse has been locked up for years."

Andrew quickly replied "We like to explore the rocks and look for things, eat our sandwiches and have 'pretend adventures' on the Island.

"O.K. Whatever makes you happy, but it sounds rather boring" said Dad. "Run along now so that I can talk to Mum and Auntie Maggie."

CHAPTER EIGHT

BUNGLE JUNGLE

Dad drove off to work early the next morning and the click of the front door woke Andrew up. He jumped out of bed to look down the garden. There was thick mist again. He shook Dudley and ran into the girls' room. They threw on some clothes and all ran downstairs, served themselves cereal and juice, left a note for their mothers and rushed down to the boat at the bottom of the garden.

Andrew grabbed the oars and Helen handed out the bright yellow lifejackets. Polly was just pushing the boat away from the end of the garden when Dudley cried

"Where are the eggs?"

"Still in the fridge. I'll get them" said Helen. She ran back up the garden and in through the back door. In the fridge, filling one complete shelf were 6 large boxes of 12 large eggs that the lady in the Farm Shop told her were only laid yesterday.

"My" she said "You be going to make a lot of omelettes with all they eggs!"

Realising that this was too big a load to be carried alone, Helen found a cardboard box in a cupboard and carefully placed the 6 boxes in it. Then she walked fast, instead of ran, back to the boat.

Their rowing was getting stronger each day and Dudley joined in to use the second set of oars in front of Andrew. The fog hung over the stream and the fields. They knew the stream bends well by now and steered a course in the centre of the steam. Out into the river, along the short stretch, staying close to the bank they rowed out into the sea. Although it was only about 100 metres to the Island they still could not see it, but the sea was calm and the rocky part of the Island was wide. They knew they would come to the rocks if the person steering held the rudder steady, without changing direction all through that 100 metres.

"There's the rock with moss for hair" laughed

Polly from the steering tiller, where both she and Helen were holding it steady. "We have to go more to the starboard."

"Wow" said Helen "You really are becoming a sailor."

"Starbucks make coffee" said Dudley

"Not Starbucks silly; 'Starboard'" Helen went on to explain to him that, if you were looking from the stern (or rear) towards the bow (front) that 'Starboard' was on the right side and 'Port' on the left side.

They turned to Starboard alongside the mossy rock and Andrew rowed a few more metres until they came to the gap where the little beach appeared. Three of them jumped off and pulled the boat up the sand until they could tie the painter rope around the rock at the top of the beach.

"Leave lifejackets in the boat and don't forget the eggs" said Andrew

"Bye Huckleberry. Wait here for us"

Huckleberry Finn, the boat, did not answer.

Andrew reached up and shook the 'grown-up alarm' bar and they quickly made their way to the hatch cover. One by one they climbed down the stone steps into the pink light of the cavern. Andrew and Dudley closed the hatch behind them. A tufty head appeared around the inside door into the Lighthouse, looked at the children and shouted behind him

"All clear Wilbur, and everyone. No grown-ups."

Turnip ran down the steps into the cavern.

"You gave us all a shock. The bells in our rooms rang and we couldn't see who it was through the spyhole because of the thick fog. Everyone went back into their rooms and locked the doors. I am so pleased it was you. Poor Freddie

Flummock is in a terrible flummox because he was washing his clothes. Now he is not sure which were the dirty clothes, which were the ones he was washing and which ones he did last week that hadn't yet been ironed."

"We are very sorry. We wanted to tell you we were coming" said Helen.

Turnip suggested that they all agree on a code of 2 rings, then a pause, then 2 rings again and then 1 ring. Then the Lighthouse people would know it was the children. They promised to remember next time.

"Well" said Turnip "You certainly have arrived at a good time. There is a Delivery Ferry arriving soon to collect Jasper Junglie and take him to Bungle Jungle. He was the one who came back with us from Great Tufty to visit his friends here for a short while."

"What is a 'Delivery Ferry?" asked Polly

"A ferry that delivers things instead of people. Just as many of your ships on the sea deliver things that you can buy that have been made in other countries. Lorries deliver if they can but, if your country is surrounded by sea, ships bring the goods. The Cola Islands are all islands so we use our Delivery Ferries to bring everything that we cannot grow or buy.

"Jasper Junglie won't have a seat on a Delivery Ferry will he?" asked Helen.

"There are a few seats – usually 3 or 4 – just behind the driver. He has booked one of these because the next ferry to the Junglie Islands may not be for several days. His ferry is not due for half-an-hour so come upstairs and have some Tea." said Turnip.

They passed Wilbur on the main steps of the Lighthouse and Polly gave him a hug.

"I've missed you" said Wilbur to Polly, and his tummy made a deep rumble as he said it.

"Here are 4 eggs for your Tea, Wilbur" said Polly

Wilbur was so pleased he kept stepping from one foot to the other and back again. His smile stretched almost from ear to ear.

"Thank you, thank you Polly. You are my best friend" he said.

"And you are the nicest, cuddliest Wilbur in the world" she replied.

"He's probably the only Wilbur in the world" said Dudley to Helen, softly so that Wilbur couldn't hear.

"Yes maybe, but there will be lots of other hairy Wilburs on their Rumbletum Island I expect. Polly will want to go there one day soon".

When they entered the Tuftys' room the children soon found out that it was not just a large circular Lighthouse room with a lift shaft in the middle, but three rooms – one on top of the other. They were linked by ladders that folded up into the floor of the room above. There were now 6 Tufties in the big room. They were Turnip, Tilly and Tania, Tania's two younger brothers Terry and Tommy, and Grandma Tulip.

"Hallo" said Helen "You were not all here when we came to Tea on Sunday."

"Yes, we were!" said Grandma "Except Tilly, who came back on the ferry with you. We were hiding in case you were not nice people. Now we know you are our friends. We were in the rooms above, being very quiet."

"Rooms above?" asked Andrew looking at the ceiling. Turnip chuckled. "A Lighthouse is very tall and this one only has three doors from the stairs into the middle section. There is a lot of space between one room and the next one high above. We have made two more rooms on top of ours. Freddie Flummock has one more and the Junglies have 4 altogether. They all have secret folding ladders that fold up to become part of the ceiling and the floor of the room above."

"That is very clever" said Andrew. "It means also that, if the grown-ups ever come in to the Lighthouse and look into the rooms, you can be hiding in the secret rooms above."

"We hope that will never be necessary" said Tilly. "Tea is nearly ready. Sit down and make yourself comfortable"

Helen said "Here is a surprise for you all" and gave Tilly an eggbox with 12 eggs in it.

"Oh Helen, they are lovely eggs thank you so much. Do you mind if I boil them now to add to the Tea?"

"Go on Tilly. They are for you to enjoy – two each"

"I will save 6 for another Tea or maybe for ferry fares. It has been weeks since we had any."

The Tufties boiled their eggs for four minutes because they were large, and then slowly ate one each, whilst the children let the scones with jam and cream dissolve deliciously in their mouths. They followed this with mouthfuls of tea (or sips in Dudley's case because he still did not like tea very much).

'Whoosh!' They all jumped and Polly spilt her tea.

"That will be Jasper going down to the ferry. Wilbur must have seen it arriving. Let's go and watch." said Turnip.

They called the lift back up to their room and then went down in it at the normal speed, not at Junglie express speed.

The rock doors were sliding apart and through the fog came a wider ferry. It was still shaped like a rocket on floats but wider than all the ferries that had been moored in Tuftytown Harbour. Jasper Junglie was waiting with his bag and two friends, who had come down to wave 'goodbye'. The ferry pulled into the side of the cavern lake and out jumped Rupert Rocket. He quickly tied the bow and the stern ropes to the posts that had been fixed to tie up boats. Rupert waved to Jasper and called to the children in his deep, manly voice

"Come down and talk to me"

All four and Turnip came down from beside the lift to meet Rupert.

"Would any of you like to go to Bungle Jungle for the day? There is a return ferry later bringing Felicity Flummock and it could collect you from Bungle Jungle."

"Yes, yes" said Dudley and Polly together

"Do you have the fare?" asked Rupert.

"Yes, we have lots of eggs in this big box" said Helen. She looked around to see Andrew running up the stairs to the inside door of the Lighthouse. He called back

"I left them in the Tufties room"

When he returned he was carrying two full boxes of 12 eggs.

"Four eggs each please" said Rupert "Return fare is the same as for going to Great Tufty"

Andrew gave him one full box and four from the other. Jasper Junglie walked slowly towards them with his bag over his shoulder and said to Rupert Rocket

"Rupert, you are soon to be a Superhero. Please can you help me.

I only have two eggs left for my fare to Bungle Jungle. I need one more egg to go from there to my home in Mungle Jungle and there is nowhere I can earn one egg in the town of Bungleberg where the ferries go. I can stay with my cousin on Bungle, but I need to go home soon"

Before Rupert could reply with a Superhero Super Scheme Helen said

"Here Jasper. Take two eggs. One can be for your fare to Mungle and one for your Tea"

"Thank you Helen. You are my Superhero today." Jasper said and grinned all over his happy green face.

Rupert looked rather sad because he was supposed to be the only person there training as a Superhero. He soon cheered up and told the children to go onboard the ferry. There were only four seats behind Rupert and Dudley counted five passengers.

"Rupert" he cried "We are one too many!"

"No problem" said Rupert in his best manly superhero voice. "There is a small seat behind me for someone learning to be a pilot of one of the rocket ferries. You come and sit there and you can help me operate the levers."

"Cor" said Dudley "I can't wait to tell my friends at school about this."

"They won't believe you" said Polly

"Yes they will!"

"No they will not. They will not believe any of our adventures were real"

"Enough!" said Rupert Rocket in his commanding manly voice.

"Fasten seat belts."

He sat down at the controls and nodded to Turnip to untie the bow and stern ropes. Andrew looked behind him. There were boxes and boxes of vegetables, bags of carrots and beetroot, trays of tomatoes and bags of potatoes piled high in the main area of the Delivery Ferry. In one corner was a package of letters and postcards and a few postage parcels. He thought that all these would be unloaded at Bungle Jungle because everyone lived in the trees and they couldn't grow crops that grew on the ground. He remembered the danger of the bigger animals that lived on the ground that Turnip had told them about when he was describing the Junglie Cola Islands.

The rocket delivery ferry moved slowly out of the rocky cavern and into the sea, then faster, and then as a plane. Rupert told Dudley to push the speed lever to 'Superfast' and 'BOOM'! Everything outside the windows became a blur. In a few minutes they found themselves landing back on water and entering a small harbour on an island that seemed almost completely covered with trees.

"We are arriving at Bungleberg town" said Rupert. "Please keep your seatbelts fastened until the ferry comes to a complete stop."

"That is what they say on all our planes when we go abroad for a holiday" said Helen, remembering the flight to Spain where the family went when she was younger.

Bungleberg was not really a town. There was the harbour with a line of market stalls near where the ferry docked, and one street with two shops in it. One shop had a sign above saying

'Post Office' and the other just said 'Store'. All around the town and the harbour was a tall metal frame that looked like a silver wall. There did not appear to be any way through this wall to the other side. Every 50 metres there was a wide wooden ramp that went from the ground and sloped up onto the top of the fence and into the branches that were hanging over it. Jasper Junglie walked beside the children as they watched 15 or 20 happy green junglies begin to unload all the goods from their ferry.

Rupert Rocket banged his chest with his fist and called out in his deep manly voice

"The return ferry will come from you at 4 o'clock. Don't be late."

Andrew waved to show him that he had heard and understood.

Jasper took them to the Post Office and, when they went inside, they discovered that it was also a café.

They sat down at one of the tables and ordered iced fruit juices because it was a hot day. Bungle Jungle was definitely a tropical island and the temperature today was over 30 degrees. The café owner was a big Junglie with a striped apron over his red shirt and shorts. He told them that the café was there for the ferry passengers to wait for their ships, or after they had had a long journey. Junglies ate mainly fruit and a few vegetables so the café could only sell slices of fruit and fruit juice. There were some delicious fruits to choose from, or to mix into drinks. The café had plums and cherries, mangoes and peaches, nectarines and oranges, kiwi fruit and pomegranates, papayas and melons, apricots and dates.

"Can you make dates into a drink, Jasper?" asked Polly

"Not really, but you can chop the into small pieces and decorate other drinks with them." answered the café owner. "They are very tasty, like tiny pieces of chocolate on a cappuccino in your country."

CHAPTER NINE

THE VILLAGE IN THE TREES

Jasper Junglie took a mobile phone out of his pocket and had a short conversation with somebody.

"My cousin and his family want us to go and visit their house."

"It would be nice to see where you Junglies live" said Andrew and, with that, they left the Post Office café just as Rupert was bringing in the parcel of letters and packages that had been on his ship. He gave them to the lady junglie behind the Post office desk.

Outside, there were dozens of junglies who had appeared whilst the children had been enjoying their drinks. More were pouring down the wooden ramps and heading towards the harbour. Andrew led the others to see what was going on. There, on the tables of the 'market stalls' were all the vegetables that had been brought by their ship. Each stall was selling a different kind of vegetable. A mass of green bodies wearing bright clothes had gathered around each stall, with the biggest crowd surrounding the potato stand.

More and more Junglies of all ages were walking and running to the stalls, whilst others had already bought some of the vegetables and were heading towards the ramps with their arms full of their purchases. Some of the people arriving were bringing fruit with them, in baskets woven from twigs and small tree branches. They were taking these to two larger stalls at one end of the harbour and selling the fruit to the people operating these stalls. Andrew went closer. The payment was in small shells that Andrew recognised. It was the shell of a winkle that he had seen in rock pools during his holidays in Devon. The Junglies were then buying vegetables with their winkles.

Jasper explained that all the money used on all the Cola Islands was winkle shells.

"I paid for all our drinks in the Post office café with two of mine" he said. "If you are very rich you can pay in eggs, but there are not many rich junglies, so we usually pay in winkles."

He told them that the fruit at the end stalls will all be sent abroad to sell, and the money was then paid for vegetables, mobiles and things that were needed on Bungle Jungle – all taken and brought by the Delivery Ferries.

Polly and Helen thought that the animals that lived on the ground must be very fierce for there to be such a strong fence built to protect Bungleberg and the Harbour. Jasper explained that there were lots of creatures living on the ground, but only two were dangerous. These were the Grumpus and the Threebee. The Grumpus is very large and has tusks and is always angry. There are only a few of them and they spend most of their time looking for other

Grumpuses and being angry because they can't find any. They are very strong and grumpy and the fence is to keep them out. The Threebee is also dangerous and we have to keep away from them by staying in the trees.

"What is dangerous about the Threebee?" asked Andrew.

"The Threebee's name is really three B's – BBB – and it stands for 'Bottom Biting Badger" said Jasper. The children all laughed.

"Don't laugh" said Jasper "They go around looking for bottoms to bite, and can give you a nasty bite if they catch you. My Brother was picking peaches from a tree near the ground and a Threebee reached up and bit him. He couldn't sit down for two weeks until his bottom had healed."

Andrew thought they had all better stay in the trees and not go on the ground at all in case they were gobbled up by a grumpy Grumpus. It would be difficult to explain to his parents if he had a bite on his bottom from a Threebee.

Jasper bought a lettuce, tomatoes and a pineapple which, because it grows in the earth and is a treat for tree people who cannot live near the ground.

"Come on, we will take these presents to my cousin's house."

They walked up one of the wooden ramps towards the top of the fence wondering how they were going to go from tree to tree. It was easier than they had thought. Many trees in jungles grow very tall to reach the sunlight and therefore their leaves shade all the lower trees and bushes.

Hanging from each of these tall trees was a rope. Down each rope, at three metre intervals was a piece of wood tied to the rope. This made a seat which you could either stand or sit on. They watched Junglies stand on a wooden piece and let the rope swing them over to the next tree, where they grabbed another rope to take them further.

Helen tried it first and the rope swung her across to a part of the next tree where two branches joined to make a platform to land on. Then each of the others swung over in turn, sitting astride the wooden pieces. Junglies helped them by holding the ropes whilst they climbed off one seat and on to the next one.

"Wheee" went Dudley as he swung over the gap between two very tall trees. "This is brill!"

The Junglies, of course, were much better at this than the children and swung like monkeys on branches as well as on the ropes. The ropes and wooden pieces were good for the older junglies, who were not as fit as when they had been younger.

"They are not ropes" said Jasper, trying to swing with two baskets of vegetables in one hand and his bag of clothes across his shoulder. They are called 'lianas' and they grow attached to the sides of the big trees.

We pull them off, take off all the leaves and tie the tops high up on a strong branch to make a kind of swing."

"It took an hour to reach the home of Jasper's cousin. They passed tree houses of different designs, all made of branches and with thatched roofs of big leaves woven together. Some were quite large with several rooms, all tied into the larger trees and resting on a place near the tree trunks that had thick branches growing out in different directions.

"These are the best tree houses I have ever seen" said Helen. "I must ask Daddy to build us one like these at home"

Jasper's cousin Julian lived with his wife and two young children in a pretty tree house with flowers growing around the doorway. He beckoned them inside and gave the children plum juice and slices of sweet mango. The little children were both staring at Dudley, fascinated by his freckles. It was the first time that they had seen freckles on a face before.

"They have only seen two humans before and think your freckles are a disease like chicken pox" said Julian. "Anyway, it is time for their afternoon nap. They have been at Playgroup all the morning and are tired"

Polly followed them out of the house and watched Julian's wife put them into little hammocks made out of thin lianas and hanging from the tree next to the house. This was the family's 'sleeping tree' where they all kept their nighttime hammocks.

Jasper hugged and thanked his cousins and they all swung on through the trees, soon coming across a part of the forest that was close to the sea.

There were dozens of lovely tree houses together, built around a central very large building that had rooms in several trees. They were all linked with rope walkways. These were similar to those Dudley had climbed on in the village playpark near his school. They slowly walked across one of these walkways and into a large room. An important looking Junglie came over to meet them. He was wearing a red hat and gold coloured shirt and shorts. Around his neck was a wide chain with a pendant hanging on his chest.

"Good Morning, I am the Mayor." he said. "You are very welcome in our village. Please stay as long as you like."

"Thank you Mr. Mayor" answered Andrew "We love your beautiful tree village. We can only stay for a few minutes or we may miss our ferry home."

"Would you like a swim whilst you are here?"

The children looked surprised.

"You have a swimming pool in the trees?" asked Polly

"Ha, ha, ha, No" replied The Mayor. "Lots of tree branches hang out over the sea down there" he pointed through the leaves to where they could see the sun reflecting off the blue sea. They could hear laughter and splashing as young Junglies played in the water and dived off a platform that was moored a few metres from the shore. There was no beach and the water was deep beside the rocky coastline.

Everybody swung through the trees of the little village, waving to people in the doorways of their tree houses. There must have been 30 houses built quite close together. Each house was made of branches and the large leaves of the trees growing around them. Palm trees provided a lot of the walls and roofs with one type of broad leaf being woven with others to make a wall, and the leaves from another type of palm tree laid on top of each other for the roof. The floor was usually of straight branches laid side by side.

Jasper and the Mayor led the children down towards the sea. The sounds of Junglies playing and swimming in the water became louder until they found themselves sitting on a large branch that was hanging over the water.

"Shall we swim?" asked Helen and, as she said it, Polly slipped and fell into the water. She came up spluttering and shouting

"It's warm. The water is warm!"

"Of course" said Jasper "this is a tropical

island and the sea is always warmed by the hot sun."

Polly began to swim out towards the platform and, when she reached it, was pulled up by two young Junglies on to the wooden deck.

"Swim if you want to" said the Mayor "I will go back to my house and fetch some towels."

Jasper and the children jumped from the tree branch into the deep water and Helen swam out to join Polly on the platform. Jasper and the boys had swum back to the rocky edge of the sea, enjoying the warmth of the clear water.

"Catch" said one of the Junglies swimming by and he threw a large piece of balsa wood to Andrew. The wood was very light in weight and it floated on the surface of the sea. Andrew leant on it and kicked his legs to move out towards the girls. The two girls and several Junglies were practicing handstands on the flat platform. Andrew swam all around the platform and back to the trees. A ladder had been made from smaller branches to make it easy to climb up on to the large branch.

For ten minutes the others swam around and then said 'goodbye' to their Junglie friends before climbing back into the trees and drying their clothes with the towels brought by the Mayor. As they began to make their way towards Bungleberg villagers hanging high in the trees called to them 'Come back soon'.

Now they all were swinging much closer to the ground and passed Junglies working in the fruit trees. Some were picking mangoes to put in the baskets made of twigs, others were working hard picking ripe cherries and some were high in palm trees pulling off big coconuts.

Suddenly, beneath them, they heard a growl

and something that went 'mutter, mutter, mutter, grumble, mutter, mutter.'

"Shhh" said Jasper "Look down there."

He pointed through the leaves at a large grey animal on the ground. It had two tusks and a wide head, four thick legs with hairy feet and a curly tail. It was definitely a Grumpus – and it had seen them! It gave out a loud growl!

"Hold on tightly" called Jasper, and all the children hung on to the branches and the ropes. The Grumpus stamped his front feet and charged their tree. His wide head bashed in to the trunk making the whole tree shake like a jelly.

"Oooh!" said Polly "I'm frightened."

Grumpus looked up again grumbling and muttering to himself.

"Let's move on quickly" said Jasper "We'll leave him behind so he can search for another Grumpus to grumble at."

They swung on through the trees and left the grumbling Grumpus, who couldn't climb trees, far behind.

Closer to Bungleberg they passed lots of other Junglies with arms laden with vegetables that they had been buying from the market stalls, One of them was limping as he made his way along the branches. He seemed to have a white bandage sticking out from his shorts and reaching a little way down each leg.

"I think he must have been caught and bitten by a Threebee and is recovering from a bite on his bottom" said Jasper

"I hope I don't get caught by a Threebee" said Helen "Are they very big animals?"

123

"No, the same size as your badgers" replied Jasper "It is just that they love to bite bottoms."

"Poor thing" said Helen

Soon they were back in the trees that led to one of the ramps, and they walked down it feeling very tired from swinging in the forest.

"I don't think I could swing on one more rope without my arms falling off" said Helen.

"You have all done very well" called Jasper "We are used to living in a forest but it is much more difficult for you, who live mainly on the ground."

They walked past more Junglies carrying vegetables.

There was a passenger ferry waiting against the harbour wall and they could see another smaller one coming into the harbour from the sea.

"The little ferry is mine" said Jasper "It will take me home to Mungle Jungle. Because it is not very far between the Junglie Islands, it doesn't have a rocket and just goes along quite fast on its skis."

The children left Jasper to meet his ferry and walked further along the Harbour wall. They were surprised to see a Lady Superhero waiting for them beside their rocket ferry.

"Hi" she said "You must be the passengers I have been told to collect. I am the Trainee Superhero who will be your driver."

Dudley said "I thought all Superheroes were men."

"Why would they all be men?" asked Polly

"I don't know. I just thought they all were. I have never heard of a lady one."

"There are five Lady Superhero trainees and one proper Superhero" said the driver

"What is your name?" asked Helen

"I will be Superhealer Sheila. When I am a full Superhero I will fly around the world to make ill people better and mend broken bones, stitch bad cuts and rescue people who have nearly drowned."

Superhealer Sheila looked good. Her brown skin glowed in the sunlight and she wore a gold sleeveless top and gold shorts over a gold bodysuit.

Her boots were also gold and fitted perfectly. She had bright blue eyes and dark hair with a white headband. On the front of her headband was a gold star with six points that shone as if there was a light inside.

The Junglie Café Owner came to meet them carrying their jumpers and the rest of the eggs

that Andrew had with him when he arrived.

"You may need these when you arrive in your country, which is not so hot as Bungle Jungle" he said

Andrew gave him two of the eggs and thanked him for looking after their belongings whilst they swung in the forest.

They waved to Jasper as they boarded their ferry. Inside there were eleven others waiting, sitting in the seats in the passenger section of the ship. Well, ten were sitting, but one, a very worried-looking lady, was walking up and down the aisle – the walkway between the two sets of seats.

"I've been so worried about you" she said to Andrew. "You and your friends have been in such danger! Did you get bashed by that terrible grumbling animal?"

"No. But we saw a big Grumpus" Andrew replied.

"And what about those dreadful badgers that run around biting bottoms? Did any of you have a painful bottom bite?"

"No. We didn't see any badgers. We did pass a Junglie who had been caught and was nursing his poor bottom" added Polly.

"I wouldn't go anywhere in this awful Junglie Island. I was worried when I heard that we were calling in here and even more worried when Superhealer Sheila told me that nice children had been visiting and exploring."

"They are fine, Felicity" said Sheila "Jasper Junglie took care of them. It is lovely here if you stay high in the trees. I often visit Bungle Jungle when I am called in an emergency to bandage a badly bitten bottom. I can fly to the scene quicker than the Jungle Ambulance can swing into action."

CHAPTER TEN

ACCIDENT AT SEA

Felicity Flummock was all in a flummox. As the rocket ferry moved away from the harbour entrance she undid her seatbelt and began walking around the cabin again.

"Please go back to your seat and secure your seatbelt Felicity" said Sheila as she started the ferry.

"Oh Dear. I have forgotten where I am going" said Felicity "Stop the ship and let me get off."

"Please sit down Felicity" shouted all the passengers together.

Felicity grabbed the steering wheel held by Sheila. Sheila hung on. There were two people steering the same wheel in different directions. The ferry was heading for the harbour wall, then for a fishing boat, then back towards the wall, and then towards ………..crunch!!

The rocket ferry stopped suddenly and pieces of wood clattered onto the passenger cabin roof and a large net folded over the starboard cabin windows.

Felicity sat down, her glasses hanging from one ear and tears in her eyes.

Superhealer Sheila quickly opened the cabin door and dived into the water. She picked one man up and flew back to the ferry handing him to the waiting passengers. He was a fisherman and was still wearing yellow waterproofs and boots. Sheila swam rapidly around large pieces of broken fishing boat near the entrance to the harbour and collected two more men from the water. She then jumped back into the ferry and began to give one of them 'mouth-to-mouth' resuscitation, breathing her breath into the man's lungs to help him breathe again for himself. The man coughed three or four times and began to breathe again properly.

All three fishermen were now sitting up and dripping water all over the cabin floor.

"You sank our fishing boat" one said to Sheila. He was a big Junglie, who may have been the captain of the fishing boat.

"It wasn't her fault" said Andrew "One of the passengers steered the ferry towards your boat."

"Well, one of you will have to buy us a new fishing boat and a new net. Ours is all torn and wrapped around the ferry. It will be useless. And it was full of fish that we had caught, worth lots of eggs."

Superhealer Sheila was talking into her wrist and a man's voice was coming out of the wrist in reply. Dudley thought she must have a new type of phone – a sort of 'armobile' – a mobile in your arm.

Seconds later two more superheroes arrived in two flashes of lightening to stand on the harbour wall, beside which the rocket ferry had now drifted. One was Zebedee Zoom and the other had a vest which said 'Wonderful Winston' underneath the big T for Trainee.

Winston was a black Superhero and he immediately began to collect all the pieces of the fishing boat from the water, borrowed a set of tools from the Harbour Master and, in only 20 minutes, had rebuilt the fishing boat. He then lifted it on to the harbour wall and emptied out a little water that was still in it. Meanwhile Zebedee Zoom had pulled the pieces of fishing net away from the side of the ferry. He took the largest piece and, outside the harbour, held on to one side and lowered the other side into the sea. He flew around pulling the net through the sea until it was nearly full of fish. After tying the two sides together he lowered the net full of fish into the fishing boat.

A large crowd of Junglies had gathered along the harbour wall to watch this amazing magic being done by the Superheroes. They began chanting 'Zebedee Zoom, Zebedee Zoom' and 'Wonderful, Wonderful Winston." The fishermen thanked them and decided to go home to change out of their wet clothes before they unloaded their latest net full of fish.

Superhealer Sheila told Zebedee and Winston that she would send a full report to the Committee on Supercola Island to help them advance from Trainees to Full Superheroes. She then spent some time calming down Felicity Flummock until she was ready to continue her journey.

Felicity was now less flummoxed and remembered that she was travelling to see her brother at the Fantastical Lighthouse. She sat next to Helen who held her hand whilst the ferry started up again and headed out of the Harbour. Soon they were flying and everything outside was a blur. Polly asked one of the other passengers whether they were also going to the Lighthouse. They were all Tufties. The ginger Tufty next to her told her that his family of four were on the way from Tiny Tufty Island to Japan. They were going to live near a town where they could watch cars being made in a factory. They could then go back to the Carrot Car Factory with new ideas to make the Carrot

Cars better. He told her that the other family of blonde Tufties were going on holiday to Spain and, at the same time, would be looking for new customers to buy butterscotch cola that could be sent in a special Delivery ferry.

Superhealer Sheila steered the rocket ferry in through the big rock doors and across the cavern lake at the Lighthouse, There was no sign of Freddie Flummock to meet his sister.

"He has probably forgotten that I am coming today" said Felicity. Helen took her hand and

headed up the stairs to the inside of the Lighthouse. They climbed the main stairs to the first room and knocked on the door. Freddie opened the door still wearing his pyjamas.

"Hallo" he said "What a lovely surprise! When did you decide to come?"

"Only yesterday you said I could stay and help you tidy your rooms" replied Felicity.

"Did I? Well I am pleased you remembered, because there is a lot to do."

Helen left them and put on her jumper. It was cold now they were back in the morning fog. The four children all went into the Tufty's room and had Tea whilst they told the tale of their adventures on Bungle Jungle, and the terrible accident when a fisherman nearly drowned. By the time they had finished their scones and cream Polly had noticed that the mist was beginning to blow away from the window in the Tufty's sitting room.

They went down to Huckleberry Finn, who was still waiting on the beach even though the tide had brought the sea halfway along the keel of the little boat. Dudley put on his lifejacket and decided to be one of the rowers. This time he and Helen rowed into the river with the help of a small red sail. The boat had a fixed mast and there had always been a waterproof bag under the seat at the stern. Andrew took out the sail with its ropes connected and pulled it up the mast. He slipped the two ropes attached to the corner of the sail into cleats (grips) on either side of the boat. The wind caught the sail and gently blew it out in one direction. Helen stopped rowing and loosened the rope on the other side and tightened the one on the sail side.

Dudley continued rowing and, with the help of the sail and the wind blowing up the river from the direction of the Lighthouse, Huckleberry moved faster than before. They continued past the entrance to the stream and up to Mr. Kerslake's slipway at the end of his long garden. The slipway was partly hidden from the main house by a boathouse and two trees. Together they stacked the oars, pulled down the sail and tugged Huckleberry up the shallow ramp next to Mr. Kerslake's own boat.

Andrew ran up the garden and told Mrs Kerslake that they were leaving Huckleberry behind and asked her to thank her husband.

The four happily dawdled their way back to the path beside the stream, crossed a footbridge over the stream and past where they had had the adventure in the hay trailer. Eventually they came to the willow tree and Stupid, who this time was sitting cleaning his face with his paw. They sat in their favourite place, side by side, dangling their feet in the water of the stream. By now their clothes were dry after the swim by the jungle. Most of the drying had happened in the warm air of Bungle Jungle as they swung through the trees.

Although they had had a long adventure it was still morning at home. The whole time in the jungle and the café had, of course, taken only ONE minute. They made their way into the house where Mum greeted them and said

"Just in time for lunch. Go and wash your hands and it will be ready in five minutes."

Dudley went to sleep with his mouth full and his head slowly settled in his plate of spaghetti bolognese. Auntie Maggie shook his shoulder and two bleary eyes looked at her from a face that dripped gravy on to his T shirt. She wiped the face with his knapkin and, with its mouth full of spaghetti, the voice said "Sorry Auntie Maggie".

Mum said "Dudley, are you feeling ill? Go along and lie on your bed. I will come up and take your temperature."

The others finished their lunch and went upstairs after Dudley. Five minutes later all four were asleep on their beds. Polly was so tired that she didn't reach her bed and was kneeling on the floor with her head resting on the bed, deeply asleep. Mum took Dudley's temperature and, by the time she read on the thermometer that it was normal, Dudley was breathing heavily in his sleep. The air that came out of his nose made a long wisp of ginger hair rise up and down on his cheek.

Mum went back downstairs noticing that Andrew had come into the bedroom, lain on his bed and gone straight to sleep.

"Maggie, you were right. Something is making our children very tired in the daytime. I don't think they are staying up during the night like you and I did sometimes in the holidays when we were their age."

"Perhaps they are playing near some of the chemicals that the farmers are using, and breathing in the fumes making them sleepy." Said Auntie Maggie.

"It is not just one child, but all four. I think we need to get to the bottom of this. When they wake up let's ask them what is going on"

The children slept for nearly three hours and

wandered downstairs one by one. It was 5pm before they had all appeared and were back at the stream, all in a line, with feet in the water. Mum and Aunt followed them outside carrying folding chairs and sat down behind them. Stupid jumped onto Mum's lap and asked to be tickled behind his ears.

"Why are you all so tired?" asked Mum

"It's very hard work rowing the boat up and down the stream" answered Helen before Dudley opened his mouth to speak.

"You take it in turns though, don't you?" asked Auntie Maggie.

"Yes, but we row all the way. At least we did until this morning when the wind came up and we could use the sail" said Andrew.

"Most children do things like that all day long and only become tired by the evening. In fact you four were running around all day when you were together last year and we had trouble persuading you to stop and go to bed at bedtime."

"I know Mum" said Polly to Auntie Maggie. "But this year we are doing so much more. Climbing stairs and the tree ropes are making us much more tired."

"You must be going into the woods and

climbing trees. You didn't mention this before. I hope these ropes are safe. Perhaps I had better come along and see." said Aunt.

"They are very safe" said three children at the same time and Andrew added "They were tied up by people who know about ropes and tree houses and things."

"O.K. then. Please be careful. I don't want any of you to break bones or hurt yourselves."

Mum looked at her sister and they folded their chairs and went up the garden to make a cup of tea.

CHAPTER ELEVEN

SOMEONE IS FOLLOWING US

"We must be careful how much we tell the Grown-ups" said Helen

They all agreed.

"We may have to stay away from the house and sleep in a barn or somewhere if we go on any more trips to the Cola Islands that take only one minute but seem like a whole morning."

Auntie Maggie and Mum were beginning to realise that the children were not telling them everything they were doing in their daily adventures. Mum began to list all the strange things the children had said

"The stream is quite a long way from the woods and Mr. Kerslake says he watches them go over to the Lighthouse on Puffin Island. When are they going to the woods? And Polly mentioned stairs as well as ropes. I have walked through the woods twice this month and not seen any ropes in the trees."

"And what is all this about eggs? Are all those they worked so hard for still in the fridge?" asked Aunt.

Mum looked "No. They have all gone. So we have 96 eggs, stairs, ropes and very sleepy children in the afternoon. I think we need to investigate."

Auntie Maggie agreed.

* * *

The next day began with rain. Breakfast was late and, whilst Polly and Dudley played a computer game, Andrew and Helen discussed the 'Cola' adventures. They decided that the next place they would like to visit would be the Island of Wilburs. How would it be possible for hundreds of enormous Wilburs to live on the same island and all have the same name? They thought perhaps that they may have numbers as well, like Wilbur 1, Wilbur 38 or Wilbur 271. How could a schoolteacher ask a question in class?

"Wilbur, what is the capital of France?"

She would get replies from 25 or 30 Wilburs at the same time.

They asked Mum whether they could borrow some CDs of dance music to take to Lighthouse Wilbur. She lent them two CDs of music from Strictly Come Dancing and two rock and roll CDs from when she was younger. The rain stopped at lunchtime and the sky cleared quickly to let the sun dry everything out. Birds always sing after the rain and their garden was full of twittering chaffinches and sparrows, singing blackbirds and cooing pigeons. Four bikes appeared from the garage and four children cycled off down the path beside the stream towards Mr. Kerslake's slipway. Just after they passed the willow tree two other figures came from the backdoor of the house dressed in green and brown clothes that would not be easy to spot in the woods and green fields.

No sooner had the four bikes disappeared around the first bend in the path than Mum and Auntie Maggie jogged past the willow tree 100 metres behind them. They could hear the children laughing in the distance as they cycled across the bridge towards the Kerslake's slipway.

"They are heading for Mr. Kerslake's house"

said Mum in a whisper that came out like a whistle because he was out of breath.

"We must follow in case they go towards the woods instead of the slipway" said Aunt as they hurried on to the bridge.

By now the grown-ups were walking fast and, because they were not used to doing this, they huffed and puffed to the next bend and were very nearly discovered! As she came around the bend Auntie Maggie turned back and grabbed Mum, They both fell backwards into the hedge beside the path. She had seen, just a few yards round the bend, Helen talking to Andrew as he fixed the chain properly on to her bike. They were talking loudly and Polly was laughing so they didn't hear Mum and Auntie squeal as their hats fell off and the brambles in the hedge scratched their arms and their brown and green slacks. They stayed still for a while in a bundle of grass and bits of hedge and arms and legs, until they heard the children in the distance.

"I have grass and burrs and sticky bindweed stuck all over me." said Mum.

"They are definitely not heading for the woods. Let's go and watch for the boat" said Aunt.

They went back down the path and crossed

back over the bridge. Then they walked towards the river, carefully keeping hidden from the direction of the slipway.

"I hope they are going to use the boat and don't go off in the other direction." said Mum.

The two ladies sat down beside another small boat that had been pulled up onto the river bank next to the place where the stream joins the river.

"I wish we had brought a flask of tea" said Aunt

After half-an-hour they could see a red sail coming towards them round the last bend in the river before it reached the sea. Mum and Aunt stayed hidden behind the small wooden boat.

"I can see Huckleberry coming this way" said Mum.

"Who on earth is Huckleberry?" asked Auntie Maggie.

"Our boat – the Huckleberry Finn. You know. We read the book in Year 6 at school. We named it after the boy in the book."

"Shhh!"

Huckleberry sailed by, helped by Helen rowing. The tide was going out and this helped them go faster because the flow of the river was heading towards the sea. Soon they reached the end of the river and went swiftly across to the tiny beach on Puffin Island.

Their mothers stood up, now with a lot of mud on their clothes, as well as the grass and the sticky bindweed.

"They are going to the Lighthouse island again. How can we follow them there?" asked Aunt.

"I don't think we can" replied Mum

The children rang the new code on the Grown-up bar. Two rings, a pause, two more rings and then a single ring. They looked up-wards and waved to the big furry creature sitting up in the light room. Wilbur waved back. In five minutes they were all inside the Lighthouse and climbing the main stairs, Flummocks and Tufties and Junglies all greeted them as they headed to the top.

"Phew. I wish we had used the lift" said Polly, as they reached the door to Wilbur's room behind the light.

Wilbur was thrilled with the new CDs and Helen's CD Player, which she was lending him. He immediately put on a rock'n roll CD and began jiggling about. He turned up the sound and climbed on to the helicopter platform and began dancing properly on the metal surface. After a few minutes he was huffing and puffing with all the effort of dancing and his tummy was rumbling like a tractor engine.

"Thank you, thank you" he said in his deep, growly voice and grinned such a wide grin that all his white teeth showed at once.

"Please can we visit your island one day soon, Wilbur" said Polly

"I don't know" he replied "I would have to go with you and I am supposed to stay here to protect all the others living in the Lighthouse"

"Don't you ever have a holiday?" asked Dudley

"Only if another Wilbur comes to replace me. I will ask the Cola Council if I can have a day off and for them to send another Wilbur. We can only travel in special ferries because we are so large" he said. "They take out all the seats and put back a few extra large ones – like arm-chairs with seatbelts. So we have to book the ferry a long time ahead. I will send a request to the Cola Council today."

*

Whilst she was trying to think of a way to get to Puffin Island Mum said to Aunt Maggie

"Did you notice another odd thing this morning? Andrew has taken some CDs of dance music to lend to someone. It can't be a child wanting music from Strictly Come Dancing, surely?"

They stayed beside the wooden boat for a while and looked towards the Island. They couldn't see the children any more. Once Andrew and the others went down into the cavern they were out of sight from the main-land. Neither of the grown-ups had an idea of how they could get across to the Island.

Then, down the river chugged a motor fish-ing boat towards the sea.

"It's Harold Burgess" said Mum. "He's going fishing. He is a member of our badminton club and we know each other well"

"Harold, Harold" called Auntie Maggie and

Mum joined in "Harry, Harry come over here please."

Harold waved back, unable to hear them over the sound of his engine.

The sisters started beckoning him to come to their side of the river.

He slowed the engine to a 'putt, putt, putt' sound, so that he could hear them.

"Harry, could you please give us a lift to Puffin Island?"

He brought the fishing boat to the river bank and Mum and Aunt stepped on board. Aunt Maggie slipped on the wet wood as she stood on the edge of the boat and nearly over-balanced into the water.

"Careful Miss" said Harold "You are not dressed for swimming."

Mum said "Thanks Harry. This is my sister Maggie. Please can you drop us off at the Island as you sail by."

"I was just going out to check my crab pots on the other side of Puffin Island. I can take you there and, after about an hour, I can bring you back if you like."

"That would be perfect" said Mum

"There is nothing there, you know. Just the old Lighthouse, of course, and a stone shack that was once used as a store. Both of them are padlocked. The rest is just rock, steep on the other side and low down on this side."

"Our children are there" said Auntie Maggie. "And we want to find out what they do on this rocky island."

"O.K. Hold tight." He increased the speed of the engine. "I'll drop you at the only stretch of beach. It is only just wide enough to take a boat, but you can jump on to the sand as the tide is nearly out."

They took off their trainers and jumped out of the motor boat as it nosed gently up onto the beach.

"Wait here and I will pick you up on my way back" shouted Harold.

They walked up the slope away from the beach holding on the rocky sides and the metal pipe that was above them.

'Ding, ding, dingaling' went the bells inside the Lighthouse. Wilbur shouted down the stairs

"Grown-ups, Grown-ups!!"

Turnip appeared from his room and went to check on the Flummocks, telling them to stay inside their room and lock the door. A Junglie expressed down in the lift with a 'whoosh' to make sure the entrance hatch into the cavern was closed down and that nobody was left in the cavern. Polly looked out of one of the windows in the side of the Lighthouse and saw two figures, dressed in brown and green clothes and hats, standing near the beach on a rocky ledge. She didn't recognise them. 'Someone was following us' she thought.

"There are two people coming and one of them could be a woman."

"Quick" called Turnip "Come inside my room and we will lock the door in case they can get inside the Lighthouse."

They all went into the Tufty's room and saw that Wilbur had climbed back into his room behind the light and locked the door.

"Did you hear the music?" said Aunt Maggie to Mum.

"No" said Mum

"It must have been the wind but it sounded like dance music. I can't hear it now."

They began to clamber over the rocky surface of the island and, as they couldn't see any of the children, thought they must have got into the Lighthouse. Mum went up the steps to the big door. It was locked with a huge padlock. From the steps they could see all the island on three sides.

There was no sign of children. They could

see a cormorant standing on the rocks with her wings open, drying them in the light breeze and warm sunshine. There were several seagulls standing and sitting in a group, one pecking at some food. The only person they could see was Harry, motoring towards a line of floats, which would be the markers attached to his crab pots that sat on the seabed under the water.

"Shhh!" said Turnip to Dudley, who was talking in a low voice.

"I think I heard them rattle the padlock on the main door. I hope they don't have a key."

"Let's go around to the other side of the Lighthouse" said Aunt

"There is a small building there."

They put their trainers back on because their feet were dry again, and they walked down a pathway towards the back of the Lighthouse. They stepped on the top of the secret hatchway and along to a white-painted stone store room built on a flat piece of rock.

"They must be in this building. There isn't anywhere else to go" said Mum

The store room was also padlocked! Aunt tried it and the padlock was securely fastened. They walked around the store. There was no window so they went back and banged on the door shouting

"Andrew, Helen. Are you in there?"

"Who do you think they are?" asked Polly to Helen.

"I don't know but they must have been following us and they will have seen our boat on the beach."

"So they know we are somewhere on the Island" said Andrew "That means that they will soon realise that, if we are not in the store or out on the rocks, we must be in the Lighthouse. They may come and break the padlock and come inside and maybe find all our friends."

"Only if one of them has blue eyes. They will only be able to see Turnip and the others if they have blue eyes" said Helen.

"I have a plan" said Andrew "If they go around to the side of the Lighthouse where the main entrance steps are we could try to go back through the hatch and run unseen to the beach, jump in Huckleberry and row back to the river as fast as we can."

"Good idea" whispered Helen "Turnip, can you watch through one of the windows over the main stairs for them to come around whilst we wait in the lift until you say 'go'"

"All right. Be careful" agreed Turnip

Polly was looking through the window in the Tufty's room and could see the two people

still knocking on the store door.

"Maggie, if they are not in here, and are not out on the rocks fishing or collecting shells, they must be IN the Lighthouse. Perhaps they meet someone inside, who is living there and likes to eat an enormous number of eggs and play lots of music."

"Then we need to get inside to check that this is a nice person and one who will be kind to the children." replied Aunt. "Come on, let's go back to the Lighthouse door."

"They are coming back towards us" said

Dudley, who was watching through the window beside Polly.

"Everybody in the lift!" called Andrew

They called the lift and sat inside waiting for a signal from Turnip, who was watching through a window on the other side. They all waited a few minutes and then Turnip came into the room and said

"I could see them coming up the steps to our main door. They both look like women."

"Bye Turnip. See you soon" said Helen and she pressed the 'Express' button. The doors closed and 'whoosh' the lift dropped very fast to the bottom of the shaft and, in a few seconds, the doors opened again. All four children almost fell over each other as they raced down the steps, through the cavern and up to the hatch door. Andrew stopped and said

"No more talking. Let's be very quiet and run as quickly as we can to Huckleberry. Duck down behind the rocks as you go. I will go last and close the hatch door" said Andrew.

"What if they catch us?" asked Polly

"We don't know who they are. They may not mean any harm. Anyway, we can probably run faster and, when we are in the boat, we may be able to row faster. Hey! How did they get to the island? They must have another boat on the beach." said Andrew. "Dudley, you go first. Look up as soon as you go through the hatch in case they have come back."

They pushed the hatch door open and Dudley looked

"It's all clear" he said in a loud voice

"Shhh" whispered all three from the steps. Followed by Helen, then Polly, Dudley crouched as he ran in the direction of the beach. Andrew tried to close the hatch gently but it still made a 'clunk' as it came down.

At the same time Auntie Maggie and Mum were rattling the padlock and shouting through the door

"Andrew, Polly, Helen….. are you in here?"

Turnip had not yet closed his door and heard them:-

'Whoever it is knows the names of our friends' he thought. He ran back to look out of his window and saw Andrew had nearly reached the beach. 'Good. They have nearly escaped' he said to himself.

Mum decided that they could not break the strong padlock. It was a mystery how the children had gone inside and for the padlock still to be fastened.

"We will have to ask Harry to help us when he returns with his crabs" she said.

They both sat down on the top step looking worried.

The children jumped into Huckleberry and pushed him away from the beach. They fixed both sets of oars. Andrew and Helen, being the oldest and strongest, began to row. Dudley pushed the boat away from the rocks and Polly steered the rudder from the stern. The two rowers were rowing together well and Huckleberry was soon 50 metres from Puffin Island and halfway towards the mouth of the river. Soon they were inside the river itself and stopped rowing for a rest.

Andrew said "Did you notice there was no other boat?"

"How did they get onto the Island? They must have come up the beach slope because they rang the alarm bell" said Helen.

They all looked back and saw two distant figures walking down the steps of the Lighthouse.

Aunt Maggie and Mum walked slowly to the top of the slope leading down to the beach, shaking their heads. They could see that Harold's fishing boat was beginning to come towards them from the place in the sea where he kept all his crab pots. They looked down at the little beach below and then exclaimed, both together

"Huckleberry has gone! It has gone. It was there when we arrived, That is very odd."

"Maybe they were swimming in the water where we couldn't see them and came back to the boat whilst we were up by the Lighthouse."

"Wouldn't we have seen a pile of clothes on the beach or on the rocks if they were" asked Auntie Maggie.

They looked out to the river and, from side to side along the coast and out to sea. There was no sign of Huckleberry or their children

Huckleberry had in fact already been rowed around the first bend in the river and, because they had not used the red sail, he could not be seen from the Island.

CHAPTER TWELVE

BE A FRIEND TO A FLUMMOCK

The four friends pulled Huckleberry up the slipway away from the flow of the river, and took the oars, the sail and the lifejackets into Mr Kerslake's boathouse in case it rained or the wind became stronger.

They mounted their bikes and rode along the footpath, across the bridge and back home. When they arrived there was no-one in the house.

Helen found the spare key in its special place and poured them all a drink.

Stupid clattered through the catflap and headed straight for his bowl of crunchy food, which he had only half-eaten earlier.

Andrew and Dudley took their drinks down to the stream and were followed a few minutes later by their sisters. Eight smelly feet dangled in the stream.

"Every time my trainers get wet they make my feet smell" said Dudley

"You should take them off when you jump in the water at the island beach" said Helen

"Your smelly feet will poison all the fish in the stream" said Polly to Dudley.

"I'll bet yours are worse than mine" said Dudley

"No they're not"

"Yes they are"

"They are not!"

"Stop it you two. We have some thinking to do" said Andrew "Why were there two ladies following us and how did they get across the water to Puffin Island?"

There was silence for a while with everybody trying to think of an answer.

"Could they be other creatures from different Cola Islands," asked Polly.

"Maybe, but they could only have come by ferry in the mist, and there was no mist today" answered Helen "And Turnip and Wilbur would have known they were coming and recognised them."

Whilst they were trying to solve the mystery Harry Burgess had brought his motor boat

into the little beach and the two ladies had scrambled on board looking windblown.

"Did you find the children before they went back up the river?" asked Harold.

"No. It is a complete puzzle where they were. The boat had gone by the time we returned to the beach and there was no sign of anyone" said Mum.

"I saw the rowing boat go into the mouth of the river ten minutes ago" said Harold.

"So, they have gone back towards the Kerslake's house then. At least they are safe."

"Yes. That is good" agreed Harold.

* * *

The eight feet began to get cold in the stream water and they were dried on an old towel that Helen found in the house when she put eight trainers in the washing machine. The children lay on the grass and thought more about being followed and also about visiting Wilbur's island one day.

After another hour two bedraggled figures staggered around the willow tree and into the garden. It was, of course Mum and Auntie Maggie. They were rather tired and fed up. All they wanted was a bath and a cup of tea. All the children together now realized who the island visitors were.

"Hallo Mum. Did you go for a walk?"

"Yes"

"You are wearing funny clothes"

"Yes"

"Why are you covered in bindweed and bits of twig. Did you fall over?"

"Yes"

"Is that mud on your slacks?"

"Yes"

"Where have you been?"

"Er…just coming back for a cup of tea" said a tired Mum.

They walked slowly up to the house with grumpy faces. Polly could hardly wait to whisper

"It was THEM. They were the ones following us. It wasn't people from the Cola Islands. It was our own mothers!"

"The strange clothes and hats must have been some sort of disguise" said Helen

The children told them later that perhaps they could have been playing on one side of the island when the Mums were on the other side, and that was why they didn't meet. The Mums said that Mr Burgess the fisherman had taken them across the water because they were interested to see where the children were going every day.

'Phew. That was close' Dudley thought.

*

It rained for the next two days and then Dad took them all to the Zoo in Paignton on the Saturday. There were no misty mornings for five days altogether until one morning Dudley woke up and crashed the blinds again. He saw it was quite foggy outside. As he had done before he rushed into Helen's bedroom and pulled the duvets off both Polly's and Helen's beds.

"It's foggy. It's foggy outside. Adventure, Adventure, Adventure!"

He jumped up and down with excitement.

The girls rubbed their eyes, then washed, cleaned their teeth and dressed in about two minutes. They gobbled down their breakfast, left a note for Mum and, in no time were cycling past the willow tree and over to Mr. Kerslake's boathouse.

"We are going to see lots of Wilburs" sang Polly, who had been dreaming of cuddling dozens of soft, hairy Wilburs.

The wind was just blowing enough to use the sail and they soon reached the little beach. 'Ding, Ding' went the bell in the Lighthouse. Twice, then twice, then once to tell everyone that it was their friends arriving.

Down by the cavern lake there were no ferries waiting, so they went up – in the lift this time – to see Turnip.

"Welcome back" said Tilly at the door. We haven't seen you for ages and wondered whether you had been caught by those people who came on to the Island."

"They were only our Mothers" said Dudley "And they didn't catch us. They just got very muddy and very tired and grumpy,"

Turnip appeared down the folding stairs from the room above.

"Today we have a trip for you……"

"To Wilbur's Island!" said Polly eagerly

"No. Not yet. That visit needs a special ferry. It is on order to bring a new Wilbur so that our Wilbur can show you his land. Today there is a visit to the tiny island of Muddle, if you want to go. That is the home of the Flummocks."

"Yes please" said Andrew. He saw the others nodding. Polly too, even though she was disappointed.

"I will come too, if you can pay my fare. We can take Felicity home."

"Do you still have our eggs in your fridge" asked Helen

"Yes. Lots of them" said Turnip.

"Whilst we are waiting, why don't all you Tufties have an egg for breakfast? We had some toast before we left home in a hurry."

"If we have eggs, you must each have a scone" said Tilly.

"Mmmm. Yes please" It was Helen. She loved the scones with jam and cream that all melted in her mouth before she could swallow them.

Five minutes later there was a knock on the door and outside was Wilbur who, because he couldn't see in the mist, had gone down to the cavern to a special screen which showed when a ferry was approaching, so that someone could open the rock doors.

"The ferry is here for the trip to Muddle" he growled "It is waiting in the cavern lake."

Turnip went to fetch Felicity as the four children made their way down to the lake. As they walked down the stairs near the Flummock's doorway they heard

"What? Now? Is it today? I haven't packed

my bag yet. Why didn't someone tell me?"

Poor Felicity was in a flummox. Everyone waited by the side of the ferry until she appeared at the top of the cavern stairs with Turnip.

The Superhero Trainee Driver was Wonderful Winston, who saluted them all by banging his fist against his chest.

"We are always prepared to wait for the Flummocks" he said in his deep manly voice. "They usually are late or have forgotten something and have to go back to collect it."

Andrew paid all their fares with some of the eggs they had left in Turnip's fridge.

"You are a kind boy" said Winston. "One day you could be a trainee Superhero too, like me."

"That would surprise my friends at school, especially as some of them are better than me at sports and schoolwork" said Andrew. "Maybe I could be a Superhero at drawing and painting – Andrew the Artist."

"You would be the first artist superhero in the world" said Winston.

Felicity was sure she had forgotten something and Polly pointed out that she was still wearing slippers. Felicity went back up to the Flummock's room in a flap and, later reappeared in high heels. These were not the best for coming downstairs or for travelling in the ferry.

Winston asked them all to take their seats in the rocket ferry and Tania Tufty untied the ropes from bow and stern so that the ship could move away from the dockside. She waved 'goodbye'. Out through the sliding rock doors and out in the sea went the ferry. Wilbur watched it move away from the Island on the special screen that could see into the mist, and then closed the doors. Faster – up on to the skis. Faster again - into the air on wings. And 'BOOM' – everything became a blur as they went 'Superfast.'

When the rocket ship slowed and came down on its wooden skis again they could see an island ahead, much smaller than any of the others they had visited.

"Welcome to Muddle" announced Winston. "I will enter the harbour slowly because the boats in Muddle Harbour will be going this way and that."

They almost needed to stop when one cabin boat motored across right in front of them. There was a lot of shouting as two other Flummock sailors in one boat collided with another, leading to a lot of chatter and confusion.

The rocket ship eventually tied up to the dockside and all the passengers stepped off thanking Wonderful Winston for a wonderful ride.

The children and Turnip sat down on a wooden seat for Turnip to be able to tell them that all the Flummocks lived on this small island, but they are so much in a flummox that they need people from other Cola Islands to come and help them. He explained that he had come with Felicity because her family lived in a house with the roof collapsing and no electricity. No-one knew how to mend the roof or fix the lights.

They took Felicity to her home which was not very far from the harbour. There seemed to be a lot of Flummocks living in the house. There were Aunties and Uncles, Grandma and Cousins, Brothers and Sisters, small and large children. The house was in a real mess with washing and ironing, books and cushions all mixed up on the chairs and sofas.

Turnip told the family that he had volunteered to 'Be a Friend to a Flummock' and had come to help them become less confused.

"Thank you Mr. Turnip" they all said

He asked Andrew and Helen to help him put tiles on the roof to stop the rain coming in and to fix a fuse in the electricity box, so that the lights came on and the cooker started to work again.

"This is wonderful" said one of the Aunties. "Now I can cook you all a meal."

The children went out into the garden, which was rather an odd garden. There were potatoes and rhubarb growing in a flower bed pansies and daffodils. One hanging basket was filled entirely with carrots. One Uncle Flummock was trying to plant a small apple tree upside down.

'Maybe he is expecting apples to grow on the roots' thought Helen

"Is it the school summer holidays here as well?" asked Andrew

"We haven't a school for the children any more" said Grandma

"The teachers couldn't remember what to teach and the children forgot where the school was. Some went to the Library and some turned up at the Police Station expecting to have classes there."

Turnip told them that the Cola Council had decided to send people from other islands to help each family get organized, and later they would send teachers to teach the Flummock children.

Auntie Flummock called them all in for their meal. They cleared the chairs and the table and sat down. First she served sausages. Then ten minutes later came some cauliflower. After another ten minutes she brought a dish of potatoes and a bowl of rice pudding. The children ate the hot potatoes and the cold cauliflower and sausages. They were just starting on the rice pudding when a jug of gravy arrived. Each of them only had a knife and fork because the spoons had all gone missing. It was quite difficult to eat rice pudding with only a knife and fork.

"Would you like some soup?" asked Auntie Flummock from the kitchen.

"No thanks" answered Dudley. Polly thought it would take all day to eat soup with a knife and fork.

Helen told Turnip that Auntie must have become rather flummoxed in the kitchen or she would have served everything in the correct order.

"That is why we need to be friends to the Flummocks. They are all very kind, but always in such a muddle that nothing is ever done properly"

"Would you like us to do some shopping for the family?" asked Helen, who had decided to be a friend to the Flummocks.

"Yes please" said Felicity. "I couldn't find any bread when I last went to the shops."

She gave Helen a handful of winkle shells to spend and Helen and Polly went out to find the shops. They turned the corner at the end of the road and could see a row of shops in the distance.

"Maybe one of those is a baker or a small supermarket that sells bread" Polly said.

They noticed that there were no cars on the road, which was quite narrow. There were only bicycles and garden rotovators towing trailers. 'Perhaps Flummocks can't drive' they thought.

Displayed in the baker's shop window was a bicycle, a wedding dress and a tray of pork chops on one side and an inflatable elephant on the other side of the door. Polly looked again at the sign. It definitely said 'Bertie Flummock – Baker.' Inside the shop were three people buying things and serving themselves using the cash register. A fourth man, wearing his jumper the wrong way round and glasses on the end of his nose, was on the telephone ordering 12 doughnuts. He was the baker and wearing a baker's hat.

"Don't you make your own doughnuts in the bakery?" asked Helen

"Not on a Sunday" was his reply

Polly thought 'Today is Tuesday'. Helen then asked for a loaf of bread.

"You'll have to go to the greengrocer. He is baking bread now because the fruit ferry has not yet arrived from Bungle Jungle."

The girls went next door to the greengrocer. One side of his shop was empty and there was a shelf of bread, some cauliflowers and children's toys on the other side. They bought two brown loaves for four winkle shells and twelve bread rolls for three more shells.

"Do you have any tomatoes?" asked Helen

"Of course not. You will only get those at the Post Office." The lady Flummock replied.

"What a muddle everyone is on the Island of Muddle" said Helen as they left the shop. They looked around. There wasn't a Post Office at all

They went into the corner shop and struggled to get along the rows of shelves because so many Flummocks were going back and forth looking for things on their shopping lists. It was, of course, a complete muddle. Shoes were next to chocolate, milk was on the same shelf as toilet rolls, and books were piled on tops of bags of potatoes. Polly found the tomatoes. Most were squashed under pots of paint, but she was able to find a few that were in good condition.

At the checkout the cash register was broken. A flustered Flummock was adding up the cost of everybody's shopping on a piece of paper.

It took almost half-an-hour to move along the queue and pay another two shells for the tomatoes.

"Let's go back now" said Polly "This shopping takes too long and she just tried to make us pay for the bread that we had already paid for at the greengrocers."

As they walked along the road two bicycles collided with each other right in front of them. The front wheels were both buckled and the two young Flummocks had to carry their bikes home.

"Where are all the cars?" they asked Turnip when they reached Felicity's house

"They would be too dangerous for Flummocks to drive and they may kill each other. Imagine what would happen at traffic lights on crossroads. The lights would be a muddle. All four would be red and everyone would have stopped. Then they would all change to green and cars would come from all four sides and have an enormous crash in the middle. The ambulance would go to the wrong place and the nurses in the hospital probably wouldn't have any bandages." He continued to say

"Because Muddle is only a tiny island the Flummocks can cycle to all the villages and, anything that needs to be carried, is taken in trailers behind those chugging little tractors that people can also use to dig their gardens.

"Let's all be Friends to Flummocks" said Andrew. "We could catch a ferry and come over to help them whenever they need it and we are on holiday with you Helen and Dudley. Turnip will be here as well"

They all agreed that this would be a kind thing to do, to help people who get into a muddle and cannot easily sort everything out.

Maybe Andrew really would become a Superhero one day.

CHAPTER THIRTEEN

MONEY ON THE BEACH

They said 'goodbye' to Felicity and all her family and walked back to Muddle Harbour. On the way they passed other strange things. There was a policeman standing outside the Police Station and Andrew asked him the time because the ferry was due at 3 o'clock. He looked at his watch and said

"I don't know, but yesterday when somebody asked me it was 7.30 in the morning."

A boy was trying to go downhill on a skateboard that only had wheels at the front. A three wheeled bicycle had an ice cream sidecar that was a freezer, but the ice cream man was taking letters and parcels out of the freezer and delivering them to houses along the road. As they walked by he gave a letter to Dudley. Dudley looked puzzled because he was not expecting to receive a letter on Muddle Island. He saw the letter was addressed to

Miss Fluella Flummock
14 Tumbledown Terrace
Muddle
Cola Islands

"I am not Fluella Flummock" Dudley called to the Ice Cream Postman.

"Ah!" he said "I thought you were. Maybe it's that man over there"

He crossed the road to give it to a man digging up the road.

Wonderful Winston was waiting at the dockside for them

"I have only just arrived. Let me have a drink before we go."

He walked over to a snack bar nearby and ordered a large 'pear and mango' cocktail. Two minutes later he was given a cup of tea, which he drank without complaining.

"Perhaps next time I will order a cup of tea and they will make me a cocktail." he laughed. "O.K. Let's go".

Everyone climbed aboard the rocket ship.

Winston called to two Flummocks to untie the ropes holding the bow and the stern of the ferry to special posts on the dockside. After much chatter to their friends one Flummock untied the bow rope and then tripped over it and fell into the harbour. The other Flummock managed to tie the rope into a much bigger knot. The bow of the ferry swung away from the side but the ship was securely fastened by the stern. Winston quickly opened the side door and climbed over the roof. He jumped off the stern, untied the rope and threw it on board, called his thanks to the Flummocks and calmly came back to his pilot seat.

"It is always a muddle asking anyone to help when we are at Muddle" he said in his deep manly voice.

Soon they were zooming through the air and everything outside was a blur.

"Turnip" asked Andrew "Why have you all come to live in the Lighthouse rather than stay in your lovely Cola Islands?"

"Hasn't anybody told you?" Andrew shook his head. "We are there to collect winkles."

"The ones with the shells that you use for money?" asked Polly.

"I spent some of them today on Muddle."

"Yes. One of the Superheroes told the Cola Council that there were lots and lots sticking to rocks along the coast of England. They decided to send us to collect them. Each of our families collect them and send them to the Council, who put them into the Cola Islands Bank, and then people can be paid their wages in winkle shells. That is why there is someone from each of the four groups of Islands in the Lighthouse – Wilbur, The Junglies, Freddie Flummock and we Tufties."

"I thought you always stayed inside the Lighthouse and only ever came out in one of the rocket ferries." said Andrew.

"I will tell you our secret if you promise not to tell anyone else – even other children." said Turnip quietly.

"I promise" said four voices, almost together.

"We can all see in the dark" he said.

"Like cats?" asked Polly

"Better than cats" replied Turnip "To us it is the same as daylight."

"Cor. That must be really cool" said Dudley "I wish I could do that."

"So, in the dark at night one of you goes out and looks for winkles?" asked Andrew.

"Usually there are four, or even six that go out

in the night-time" corrected Turnip. "Inside the cavern there is a room that we have cut in the rock that has rock for a door and is very hard to see. Inside this room we keep a boat like yours. We bring it out on to the lake after dark and take turns to sail in it. We go out through the sliding rock doors and sail along the coast to the some of the beaches. Then we collect bags of winkles from the rocks. We take them back to the Lighthouse and cook them for our Tea, putting the shells in boxes to send back on a special Bank Ferry to the Cola Council on Supercola Island.

The rocket ferry landed in the mist and motored on the skis into the lake and through the big sliding rock doors. Wonderful Winston waved 'goodbye' and went out to sea again before Wilbur closed the doors.

"Come. I will show you the secret door in the rock" said Turnip.

It was only a few metres from where they were now standing. They could hardly make out the gap where the door met the rock face because the door was cleverly cut in the same rock. Turnip pushed the centre of the door and it slid back and then sideways behind the front wall to reveal a room in which stood a boat that was a little longer than Huckleberry.

Beside it was a mast lying on its side and two bags which probably contained sails. The boat was on a metal trolley with a handle and two wheels, one on each side. Inside the boat was a square box in the centre which contained a motor.

"It's a motor boat" said Andrew.

"The motor is only for emergencies if we are discovered and have to make a quick getaway. We usually only use the sails and paddles."

"I'd love to come with you one night to help you find your money on our beaches" said Andrew quietly to Turnip, who whispered back

"Come anytime if you can. It may be difficult for you to come at night in case your parents find out and are worried about your safety."

"Maybe I can one night soon. How do you

get someone as large as Wilbur into this boat?"

"Wilbur always stays on guard back here. He operates the sliding doors and keeps watch. That is why he is often asleep in the daytime" added Turnip.

"Will you go out tonight?" asked Andrew

"Yes, if there is no fog" replied Turnip

"Can I come?"

"We will start early, as soon as it's dark. We usually go for two or three hours. If you come at 9 o'clock we can be finished by midnight. You can meet us by the wooden post at the place you used to leave your boat when you first used your bicycles to come and visit us. The tide is low tonight."

"If I don't come tonight it will be because I cannot leave the house without being discovered. Wait for half-an-hour and, if I have not arrived, go without me" said Andrew.

They stayed in the Lighthouse for the rest of the morning because it had only been 10am when they returned from Muddle. This time they had Tea with the Junglie family with lots of fruit that had been brought over from the Jungle Islands.

"This Junglie Tea is better for us than scones and jelly and ice cream" said Polly.

They talked to the Father of the Junglies about the bags of winkles. He was called Jeremy and he explained that each family group in the Lighthouse was collecting bags and boxes that would go back to the Cola Islands Bank and would be then sent to their own islands. Junglie bags for the Jungle Islands, Flummock bags for Muddle, Tufty bags for the Outer Tufty Islands and Wilbur bags for Rumbletum Island where all the Wilburs live.

Jeremy's wife, Jessie, went on to tell them that the families had already collected many bags of winkles and the piles in the store room were large for Junglies, Tufties and Wilbur. Wilbur is the 'lookout' and our sliding door operator for us all, so they put one bag on his pile out of every four they collect.

Juniper, a teenage girl Junglie in the family, said

"There is a problem with Freddie Flummock. He has only collected two bags in all the time he has been here and can't remember where he put them."

She went on to tell them that there were supposed to be four Flummocks living in the Lighthouse, but the others kept missing the ferry or forgetting they should be in the Flummock Money Team. Jeremy added

"Turnip Tufty and I have decided that, from tonight onwards, out of every four bags of winkles that the Junglie and Tufty families collect one will go to Wilbur and another will go to Freddie Flummock. Then he will not be so worried and flummoxed.

"That means you are giving away half the winkles you are finding" said Dudley, showing that he was good at Maths.

"They are our friends and it is a good way to 'Be a Friend to a Flummock'"

"Would you like to have one of our stickers?" Juniper asked. She gave a bright yellow sticker to each of them. It was 5 centimetres across and round, and had black writing on it that said 'I've been a Friend to a Flummock'. The children all peeled the back strip off their labels and stuck them on to the front of their T shirts. Then they said 'goodbye' and 'thank you' to the Junglie family and got into the lift. Dudley pressed the Express button and 'whoosh', the lift shot down to the cavern in a few seconds, leaving the feeling that their tummies were still up on the Junglie level. The pink lights were still on in the cavern and the lake reflected the pink lights on to the rock ceiling.

Soon they were back in Huckleberry and

sailing up the river to the slipway. The mist had all blown away to let the sun shine on their backs as they cycled home across the bridge and past the willow tree. There was no sign of Stupid as they put away their bikes. Andrew was last and left his outside against the garage wall without the others noticing.

They spent the afternoon further down the stream, lying on towels on the bank and talking. Then they slept for an hour and watched the flowing water of the stream to see whether there were small fish swimming there. Polly watched a chaffinch standing on a stone at the edge and drinking the cool water. She then saw two robins squabbling over a piece of biscuit that she had throw them. It hardly seemed that already today they had had an adventure on Muddle amongst the Flummocks. What a good holiday this was becoming – the best ever.

"I hope we get a chance to go to the Land of Wilburs" she said.

"Wilbur is your favourite isn't he?" asked Helen

"I like them all. Except the Grumpus. I think they are the nicest people I have ever met. Most grown-ups only talk to you for a few minutes and have to go away and do something else. Tufties and Junglies and Flummocks will answer all our questions and give us lovely trips and new things to eat and drink. But Wilbur is the only big cuddly one with warm long hair."

"Perhaps on the next misty day the Wilbur ferry will come and take us to Rumbletum Island" said Helen as they all began to get up to go back to the house.

Just as they moved there was a 'splosh' right in front of them. A trout that seemed to be about 20 cms long swam to the surface and gobbled up a large fly that was sitting on the water. His body came half out of the stream and his mouth closed over the fly before he flopped back under the water again.

"I've seen a fish" said Dudley "I knew they were there."

"If you didn't make so much noise you would see more of them" said Polly.

"It's easy for you. You can sit all afternoon in the sun looking into the water and see the fish. Your skin is going brown already. I have to stay in the shade most of the time because I have ginger hair and my skin burns and goes all red. It's not fair!"

"One day you will go as brown as me. You have so many freckles. Maybe they will all grow together and you will have a tan too."

"Ha, ha, very funny" said Dudley with a grumpy expression on his face.

"Stop it, you two. It is time for us to go inside for tea. Pick up all your litter and bring it to the house with you. Then the stream bank will still be beautiful when we come here again." Helen was giving the instructions this afternoon because Andrew had a reason for sleeping on the grass for longer than the others.

"Wake up Andy. We are going home now." She said.

After the evening meal with Mum, Dad and Auntie Maggie the children all went to bed before 7pm.

"There is definitely something unusual going on. Children on school holiday don't go to bed so early unless they are ill" said Mum. "Ray, do you think we should call the doctor?"

"They all seem O.K. to me, but I agree it is very strange. Perhaps all the fresh air and sunshine is making them more tired than usual. Sea air affects some people like that, you know."

"I understand, Ray, but we live here all year round. I could accept it if it was only Andrew and Polly but they are all fast asleep every day by 7.30pm" said Mum looking as worried as a Flummock.

If she knew the true story she may be even more worried.

"We tried to follow them to find out what they were doing and got into a tangle ourselves. We came home wet and muddy and covered in bits of hedge." said Auntie Maggie.

You two would be no good as detectives" said Dad as he left the room.

Later that evening, whilst they were watching a film on television, they didn't see a figure in the shadow of the moon heading for a bike that had been left against the wall of the garage. Andrew had checked that Dudley was fast asleep and opened the bedroom window. The window was beside a tree with branches that grew close to the house. He climbed on to a thick branch and down the tree to the ground.

The only person who knew his secret was Stupid, who had decided to go exploring in the moonlight and came out of his catflap, giving Andrew a shock as he crept past the back door.

CHAPTER FOURTEEN

ANDREW'S PRIVATE ADVENTURE

Without turning on his cycle lights Andrew pedalled fast by the light of the Moon along the stream path towards the river. He surprised several rabbits that were chewing the grass that grew alongside the stream bank, and nearly ran over one of the babies which was slow to get out of the way. He knew it was past nine o'clock and hoped the 'winkle boat' would wait for him.

The bike whizzed around the last bend before he reached the mooring post. The boat was still there with Turnip holding on to the wooden post to keep it steady. With Turnip Andrew could see another Tufty and two of the Junglies that he had watched over a week ago swinging on ropes in the cavern. He let the bike fall onto the grass and knew it would be safe until he returned. No-one would come along the path in the dark for a walk.

The he heard a voice behind him:-

"Wait for me. Wait for me!"

"Who is that?" asked Turnip "Quick, jump in the boat. We mustn't be seen."

Another bike came around the bend in a cloud of dust and the rider called out:-

"Don't go. It's me, Helen!"

Turnip grabbed the wooden post again to pull his boat back towards it.

"Andrew didn't say you were coming too." he said.

"I didn't know" said Andrew

Helen jumped on board after Andrew puffing and panting after her fast bike ride.

"How did you know I was coming to join them tonight?" said Andrew.

"I heard you talking to Turnip earlier. Then I watched from my bedroom window. When I saw your moonshadow come across the grass towards the garage I climbed out of my window on to the garage roof and down to the ground, took my bike from the garage and tried to catch up.

Phew, I cycled faster than I ever have because you went so fast. Now I am completely puffed out."

"Can Helen come too please Turnip?"

"It will be a squash and as many as we can fit into the boat."

All the others were saying "Yes", so Helen joined the winkle team.

They raised the mainsail and the jib, which was already fixed and was tightened by pulling the rope on one side. A gentle breeze took the sails and blew the boat along the coast away from the mouth of the river and Puffin Island.

Turnip was steering and the Junglies were looking after the sails.

After sailing for one kilometre along the coast, which Andrew and Helen could only see in the moonlight and the Junglies and Tufties could see clearly, Turnip steered the boat towards a beach that was edged by rocks and rock pools. He sailed up on to the beach and stopped with a shudder. A Junglie jumped on to the sand and ran a little way up the beach with the anchor, which he pushed into the sand. This and its attached rope would stop the boat from washing back into the sea.

There was a pile of empty cloth bags in the bow. Each person took one and headed for the rock pools.

"We can only do this at low tide" said Turnip.

Helen explained to Andrew that the tide came in and out twice every day, and usually about an hour later each day than the day before.

"The winkles will be above or just below the water line at low tide, but too deep to reach when the tide is full" explained Turnip.

They all began to move around the rocks knee deep in the water or paddled in the rock pools searching for the winkles that were clinging to the rocks like small snails on a garden fence. Helen and Andrew couldn't find them as quickly as the Cola Folk because they had to use the moonlight. The moonlight created shadows and it was only possible to see the winkles if they were not in the shadow but, of course, the Cola Folk could use their night eyes to see everything.

It took Andrew and Helen an hour and a half to fill their bags. By this time each of the Cola Folk had two full bags to take back to the boat.

Whilst they had been searching, the tide had come up the beach and the boat was floating. The anchor, dug into the sand, stopped it from floating out to sea. Everyone had very cold legs and feet and they were pleased to climb out of the water and begin sailing again.

It was lovely sailing, with the moonlight shining a white path on the surface of the sea. The cliffs and rocks loomed black or grey as they travelled back along the coast. Andrew said to Helen:-

"If we come again we will need torches so that we can find the winkles more easily."

"Turnip, we would like our bags to go to Freddie Flummock"

Helen had been reading the words on the label that was still stuck on Andrew's T shirt. "That means you and the Junglies will not have to give him two of yours and there will be more for your islands."

"Thank you. We have four – one for Wilbur and three for us. The same with the Junglies. Freddie will be a happy Flummock when we tell him. He was still looking for his two bags when we left the Lighthouse this evening. He should really be out with us tonight.

"They approached Puffin Island and could see the Lighthouse looking enormous in the moonlight. As they looked across the island there was the shape of a man walking along the rocky path from the store to the little beach. Helen was the first to see the man:-

"There is someone on the island"

Turnip and the others looked with their clear eyes and could see it was a man. The Junglies quickly dropped the two sails so that the boat slowed down whilst they watched. Another man followed the first one. One of the Junglies pulled the jib sail up again and the light breeze took them into the shadow of the rocks at the side of the island where they could see anyone leaving from the beach.

They all waited quietly until they saw another boat head out from the beach. Its motor went 'chugg chugg' as it headed for the river mouth.

"I hope they don't see our bikes" whispered Andrew.

"They are going up the river, away from where you left the bikes" said Turnip

"What were they doing on our island in the middle of the night?" asked Helen.

"They were here before, about a month ago, also in the night. The bell rang at one o'clock in the morning when we were all asleep. Wilbur watched them and Tania could see through our window. They went to the store and had a key for the padlock. It was high tide and we couldn't collect winkles that night so we were all inside."

"Did they go into the Lighthouse?" asked Andrew

"No. They put some boxes into the store and went away again. We hoped they wouldn't come back."

"Maybe they are smugglers" said Helen "The store is a good hiding place. Hardly anyone comes to Puffin Island now. It is padlocked and I don't think there are any windows to see inside."

The sound of the motor boat faded in the night air. The Junglies pulled up the mainsail to let the wind blow their boat across to where Andrew and Helen had thrown their bikes into the grass beside the towpath. Turnip thanked them for their help and the two children stepped off the boat.

"We'll give the two bags of money that you collected to Freddie when we go into the Lighthouse" he said.

The Junglies and Tufties sailed around the island and in through the doors to the cavern lake. Wilbur was waiting and told them that he had been watching the two men come ashore and carry more boxes into the store. He thought another man was waiting in their motor boat.

The Cola people all met early the next day and decided that Wilbur should make a sign and hang it high up on the helicopter platform if the men came again when they were out collecting the winkles. They also thought they needed to be careful in case the men were dangerous. They must be crooks if they only came at night and never in the daytime.

"If one of them has blue eyes and sees us we could have problems," said Jeremy Junglie.

Meanwhile Helen and Andrew found their bikes in the grass and cycled back home more slowly than they had come. They watched a big fox walking across one of the fields as they rode along the path beside the stream.

"That is why we have not seen any rabbits on the way home," said Helen "They could smell the fox and are hiding in their burrows because they don't want to be Mr. Fox's dinner tonight."

They quietly put their bikes against the garage wall. Helen couldn't find a way to climb back on to the garage roof. The Moon had moved around the sky to shine on that side of the house. Even if she had been able to get back

on to the roof of the garage it may have made a noise. Anyone hearing the noise and looking out of their window would have seen her in the moonlight.

So both of them climbed the tree on Andrew's side of the house and in through his bedroom window. Dudley was still fast asleep with one arm hanging out of the bed and his hand resting on the floor. Andrew lay on top of his bed and Helen crept along the landing to her room and into her cosy bed.

They lay for a while, each thinking about strange men in boats and walking on their island, about winkles and moonlight and dark blue sails, foxes and rabbits and nighttime adventures. A few minutes later they were both fast asleep. Only Stupid knew they had been out. He had seen them going, nearly colliding with Andrew by the back door, and he watched them return – from his place hidden in the dark behind the willow tree.

CHAPTER FIFTEEN

THE ISLAND STORE ROOM

Helen was first to wake up in the morning. She looked out of the window to see whether it was misty. Everything outside was clear and the birds were welcoming a new sunny day. She went back to bed and slept for another two hours. Polly and Dudley had finished their breakfast before Helen and Andrew joined them at the table.

There was a message for Andrew from Derek Brown, the Builder, who had given them jobs to do when they were earning money to buy eggs. The message simply said 'I have more jobs to be done, if you want them' signed Derek Brown.

Andrew said "Let's do some more jobs and buy more eggs to give our friends. Not so many this time. Dudley and I can go to Mr. Brown and you girls could see whether Mrs Walker needs more shopping."

They agreed and set off immediately because it was already 9.30am.

Mr. Brown was pleased to see them:-

"I am very busy today and need to take timber and paint and 100 of those bricks to a house this afternoon. Two of my men have to build an extra room and another man will do some painting. Can you please bring them out beside the road so that the lorry can pick them up at midday"

"Yes" said Dudley "We can do it."

Mrs Walker was also pleased to see Polly and Helen again. This time she gave them some money and asked them to catch the bus into Sidmouth and buy about 20 items of shopping in Waitrose.

By lunchtime both pairs of children had completed their jobs and earnt £4 (£2 for each person).

After lunch they went down to the Farm Shop in the village and each bought an ice cream for 50p and spent £6 on eggs.

"My goodness, it's you again buying eggs" said the shop lady "You must be doing a lot of cooking, or perhaps all your relatives are staying for a week."

"We are giving them to people who like eggs for breakfast, but don't have any" said Polly.

"Well, well. That be very unusual and be very kind" said the lady, looking rather puzzled by Polly's reply.

They all then decided to go to see Jeremy Junglie or Turnip Tufty to find more about all the money they were collecting and storing in the Lighthouse. There was very little wind in the afternoon so they had to row most of the way down the river. Huckleberry was pulled up the beach and the code rung on the 'Grown-up's Alarm'. Twice, then twice, then once.

Wilbur waved from his glass room in the old light. Polly waved back and blew him a kiss.

Turnip met them in the cavern and asked whether they would like to see the money store. They all climbed into the lift and Turnip pressed a button. The lift stopped between the Flummock's Room and the Tufty's Room. The doors opened and they were faced with a single door. Turnip put a key in the door lock and opened the door. He switched on a light. It was a small room and only contained bags of winkle shells in heaps around the floor. Each heap had a name behind it – Wilbur, Tufty, Junglie and Flummock.

The two largest heaps were 'Junglie and Tufty', then Wilbur had about half of theirs and only two bags for Flummocks. Dudley then said

"It's not fair. No-one is being friendly to the Flummocks" and he pointed to his badge.

"Well, we have just started" said Andrew "Two of the bags collected last night have been given to Freddie and, if he can find the other two he collected himself, there will be more." Andrew didn't mention that he and Helen had had an extra adventure last night.

The lift took them up to the next floor which was the Tufty Room.

Of course Tilly was waiting with a delicious Tufty Tea. It was laid out on a table for all the children and Tufties to enjoy. The scones melted in their mouths and everyone drank the tea, except Dudley who only had two sips. Helen gave Tilly a dozen eggs as a present and all the Tufties eyes lit up as they were thinking of boiled eggs for 'breakfast tea' tomorrow morning.

"Turnip, how can you have both eggs and winkles for money?" asked Dudley.

"Winkle shells are our main money – money that we use all the time. Because none of the Cola Islands can keep chickens and we love to eat their eggs people will always accept eggs as payment as well. One egg is worth 20 winkle shells. Eggs will go bad if you keep them too long, so the people who take eggs for payment have to spend them quickly or eat them for their tea."

Tania then said "We have been moving our belongings into the rooms above our sitting rooms this morning. That is why there are only a few chairs and a table down here. It is because the two men we saw last night may have a key to the padlock and come into the Lighthouse and find us."

"You saw two men last night?" asked Polly

"Yes, Wilbur saw them and so did I. We think there were three, but one stayed in their boat. It was while the winkle team was out and had sailed along the coast. They brought big boxes and put them in the store room down there" she said, pointing out of the window to the white stone store below.

Everyone decided to go down and investigate. 'Whoosh' went the express lift and they walked through the cavern and up through the hatch and along the path to the store room.

"We heard the 'Grown-up Alarm' and Wilbur told everyone to hide.

I stayed near the window and saw them come to the store room. They had a key to the padlock and put the boxes inside. They came out again very quickly, padlocked the door and went back to the beach" Tania told them. "Dad saw them motor away up the river when he was sailing back. They came once before, four or five weeks ago, and did the same thing."

"Did they go into the Lighthouse?" asked Polly

"No, they just came to the store and went away again."

"I wonder what was in the boxes" said Helen.

She didn't say that she and Andrew had also seen them because she thought that Polly and Dudley would be upset if they knew they had not been part of the moonlight adventure.

"Probably things they are smuggling abroad, or are receiving from abroad against the law" said Turnip

"I wish we had a key to go inside and see what is there" said Andrew.

"When they left one of them put something under one of the rocks beside the path" Tania said as she began to look. "I wonder if it was the padlock key"

They all began to search under pieces of loose rock around the front of the store and along the path. Underneath they found beetles and ants and lots of mud, but no key. A frog jumped out from under a big stone and hopped away across the rocks.

"Help me lift this one" said Tania "You are bigger and stronger than me Andrew."

Andrew lifted the frog stone and there, underneath, was a large brass key.

"Good. Now we can go inside and see what they are keeping there," he said.

"Do you think they could be watching us through a telescope from the mainland" asked Dudley.

"No, I don't think so. There are only a few houses along the river and they went a long way upstream" answered Andrew.

Andrew turned the key in the padlock and it unlocked straight away. He opened the door and went inside. On one side there was a pile of jumbled up old fishing nets and floats, two circular crab pots and some coiled ropes. Stacked on the other side were several boxes. They were large and quite heavy.

"Maybe they are full of guns" said Dudley

There is some writing on one of them. The

box was upside down so they had to turn it over to read it. In black capital letters was written

Best Competition Tennis Racquets

Made in New Zealand

There was another with writing at the back of the stack. They dragged the box out. This one had printed on it

Running Shoes

Approved by The German Athletic Association

"These are boxes of sports equipment" said Helen "To bring them at night must mean they have been stolen."

"Or brought into the country without paying Customs Duty or Taxes" said Turnip, who knew about these things.

They pushed the boxes back in the stack and came out of the store.

Then put the padlock back on and placed the key under the same stone that it had shared with the frog. Turnip, Tania and Polly sat down on flat rocks, whilst the others stayed standing.

"I think we should tell the Police that there are these boxes in the store and they are brought here at night" said Helen.

"If the Police come they will want to search the Lighthouse as well. They may find us if they do" said Turnip with a worried expression.

"We must not let them do that" added Andrew. "And the men may be innocent. The boxes could belong to them."

They decided to do nothing and for Wilbur to be extra watchful at nights, and be ready to signal if the men came while the winkle boat was still out collecting winkle money.

All the way home the children discussed the storeroom men and the winkle money.

"If I brought home some winkle shells do you think I could buy sweets with them?" asked Dudley. Everyone laughed.

"You could try, but I think Mr Drew in the sweet shop would tell you not to be silly" said Helen.

Inside the house Dad had left his morning paper on a chair in the sitting room and the headline read 'Another Sports Shop Raided'.

'In Exmouth' the article printed 'a sports shop was burgled yesterday evening and a quantity of expensive running shoes was taken, as well as football boots and trainers. This is the third sports shop in the region to be raided in the last two months. Police are looking for three men, two with black hair and one with blond hair and striking blue eyes'

Andrew read this aloud to Helen and Dudley. Polly had run upstairs at the time.

"This proves the goods we found are stolen. They must have brought them to the store straight after the burglary."

"What can we do?" asked Helen "We can't contact the Police in case they discover our friends." said Helen "If we tell Daddy he will go to the Police, and we can't really tell him either because he will also have to know about all the Cola people."

CHAPTER SIXTEEN

RUMBLETUM ISLAND

The very next morning it was misty again. Not as thick as before. They all thought there was a chance a ferry may come in if they raced along and cycled and sailed at top speed. By now they knew every bend and obstacle along the path and over the stream bridge to Mr. Kerslake's slipway. They zoomed into his boathouse to leave their bikes and launched Huckleberry quickly. Dudley fixed and raised the sail as Andrew and Helen both took oars to row and Polly sat in the stern, fixed the rudder and began to steer.

The tide was going out and this helped them, together with the flow of the river, to reach the little beach in record time. The mist was thin.

They could see about 50 metres and they hoped a ferry would come.

After running along the path and down through the secret hatchway they were surprised and pleased to see a ferry waiting at the side of the rocky platform in the cavern. Standing beside it was Wilbur and Turnip – and another Wilbur with darker brown hair, just as tall and as big as their Wilbur.

Polly ran to Wilbur for a welcome cuddle and he said

"Hallo Polly, hallo everyone. This is Wilbur Lampshade who has come to be the Lighthouse Watchman whilst I am showing you my Island." There was the rumbling sound of a very noisy tummy and Wilbur Lampshade greeted them in a growly voice and with a big white smile. Helen had forgotten that all the Wilburs had lovely white teeth.

The door at the top of the stairs opened and a new Superhero appeared. He came down the stairs three at a time and took one leap from the bottom stair to land beside Andrew. He banged his chest with his fist in salute and said in a deep manly voice

"Good Morning everybody. My name is Toby Tornado and I am in charge of this special Wilbur Ferry."

"Good Morning Toby" said Dudley, thinking that this was another good day, being able to meet yet another Superhero to tell his friends about at school. They would not have heard of any of them because they were Superhero Trainees who had not yet done anything super special to be in a film or on TV.

'Of course they will believe me' he thought, remembering what Polly had said the last time he had mentioned telling his friends.

"All aboard" said Toby "We must leave before the mist clears, or the ferry will have to stay until it is misty again."

Inside the rocket ferry there were only eight passenger seats, each one twice the size of the seats the children had sat in before. Wilbur sat in one. Andrew and Helen took one each, but Polly and Dudley sat in the same seat and wrapped the seatbelt around them both.

Toby Tornado was driving or flying the rocket ferry and he closed the door and waved to Turnip to cast off the bow and stern ropes, letting the ferry go out through the sliding doors into the mist. Wilbur's tummy was rumbling more than ever with the excitement of a few days at home with his friends. As the rocket increased in speed and began to fly the engine noise drowned out Wilbur's tummy.

Toby spoke into his microphone:-

"Welcome to the Wilbur Ferry" he said "Today we will fly directly to Rumbletum

Island where Wilbur Lemonade lives. This is one of the two Wilbur Islands and is smaller than Great Bear Island, which is a little further to travel.

"Are you Wilbur Lemonade?" Polly asked Wilbur.

"Yes."

"And the new Wilbur in the Lighthouse is Wilbur Lampshade?"

"Yes. We all have a second name. It would be difficult otherwise on Rumbletum Island."

"We thought so" said Polly " And we were trying to work out how a teacher could ask someone a question in class when everyone had the same name. Also your names are funny names aren't they?"

"When we first are born" Wilbur replied "The baby Wilbur is named after the first thing his mother sees."

"Ha, ha, ha. That is definitely funny" said Dudley "Wilbur Lemonade and Wilbur Lampshade. Ha, ha, ha"

"Don't laugh at him" said Polly "It's not his fault they have different names to ours."

"You are right, Dudley. There are some funny names on my Island." said Wilbur. "When I was born I was a very small bear and my Mum saw a glass of lemonade, so I am Wilbur Lemonade. Some of my friends are called Wilbur Doctor, Wilbur Sandwich, Wilbur Goldfish and Wilbur Wellington Boots."

"I want to meet all your friends" said Polly "and cuddle each one."

The backs of the seats contained a scone, cream and jam, just as on the ordinary passenger ferries. However these were huge, Wilbur-sized scones. Andrew took his and decided to share it with Helen because it was so large. Polly and Dudley shared theirs too.

Soon the skis of the rocket came down and they landed on the water.

Toby Tornado closed the wings and they gently came alongside a long jetty that was like a wide wall. It stretched out into the sea from a small town of very large houses.

"I will wait for you here this afternoon at about six o'clock" said Toby and went off to deliver an urgent message to the owner of a house near the jetty.

Wilbur explained that, on this island, there is only one road. It went all around the coast from village to village. If they wanted to go inland Wilburs had to walk across the fields or along pathways. The buses came by every 20 minutes and drove along the road round and round the island.

Anyone who wanted to travel to the next village just got on the bus. Other buses went around the other way. When Helen saw the bus coming she could hardly believe how big it was. She supposed it had to be so big for the Wilburs to be able to get in and be able to sit down.

They climbed on board and Wilbur paid some winkle shells to the driver.

"Take us to Seagull Village please" said Wilbur to the Driver Wilbur.

'That will be two winkles for you and half price for your half-sized friends – six winkles in all. He gave Wilbur an extra large bus ticket for each of them. They say down on the huge seats and smiled at all the other Wilburs on the bus, who smiled back showing lots of white teeth.

There were no cars on the road, only a few bicycles. Because there were no other roads crossing this one there were no junctions or traffic lights to slow them down. The driver had to watch out for pedestrians or for bicycles, but he could usually keep the bus going without stopping until the next time a passenger signalled.

"The bus is stopping anywhere" said Dudley "Not just at special bus stops."

You are right. It will stop anywhere a passenger wants to get off or, if someone waves from the roadside, so they can get on. We only have real bus stops in the centre of each village." said Wilbur "And, if we miss a bus, another one comes along in 20 minutes."

Andrew was looking out of the window at a field next to the road that seemed to have ostriches in it. He pointed to them and Wilbur said:-

"Chickens cannot live here or on any of the Cola Islands, but ostriches can. They lay Wilbur-sized eggs for us to enjoy."

"Have you ever eaten an ostrich egg, Andy?" asked Helen

"No. I'll bet it would make a super omelette. Maybe we can try one here."

It took about half-an-hour to drive to Seagull Village, and they got off the large blue bus in the village centre. Together they began to walk along a street towards the back of the village, past several big houses.

Happy, hairy Wilburs greeted their Wilbur in the street or from their gardens. "Welcome home Wilbur", "Nice to see you back again", "Did you enjoy your competition prize?", "Hallo Wilbur. This is a surprise. Are you on holiday?"

Wilbur replied to everyone and the children saw how popular he must be in the village. They walked past a bigger building that was a hospital.

"This is the first hospital I have seen in the Cola Islands" said Helen.

"It is the main hospital on Rumbletum Island" said Wilbur "Many of the Wilburs living in the village are doctors or nurses who work in the wards. All the dentists have left the Island because our teeth are so good, but we still need doctors and nurses when we are ill or hurt."

Not far from the hospital was Wilbur's house. The doorways and the ceilings, the tables and chairs were all twice the size of those in Dudley's home, and the glass of milk that Wilbur's Mother gave him to drink was twice as much as he would normally be able to drink.

Wilbur's Mother and Father were very pleased to see their Son after his long stay at the Lighthouse.

"We are very proud of him, collecting the money for the Wilbur Bank. Only special Wilburs are given that job" they told the children.

"He is a very good watchman" said Polly "And my very favourite person in all the Cola Islands"

Wilbur's Mother laughed and patted her on the head.

"Would you like some lunch?" asked Wilbur's Father. "We call it Lunchtime Tea here but it is lunch in your country."

"Yes please" said Helen, who seemed to always be hungry on this school holiday.

"We are all having porridge. Will that be all right for you?" asked Wilbur's Mum.

"Wonderful" replied Polly. "You are all like big, friendly Teddy Bears and I know that bears love porridge. Mummy used to read us the story of Goldilocks and the Three Bears, which was partly about the porridge they ate for breakfast."

We are not quite like Teddy Bears, but we probably eat the same food. We grow lots of oats in the fields and most Wilburs eat porridge or oatcakes or flapjacks at some time every day."

"I love flapjacks" said Dudley to Wilbur's Mum.

"Then I will send you home with some later" she replied.

She served a steaming bowl of porridge to each of the children and a huge bowl for Wilbur. They put milk on the top to cool it and Dudley and Polly added some sugar. Wilbur finished his very quickly because he had not had porridge for a long time and had missed it. He got up from the table because his tummy rumble was making it difficult for the children to hear each other speak. Wilbur's Dad sat down in the chair, looked at Wilbur's empty porridge bowl and said

"Who's been eating MY porridge?"

Everyone laughed.

"My wife and I were going to the Annual Wilbur Games this afternoon along the coast at Paradise Bay. There will be lots of sports and races and good things to buy and eat. Would you like to come?"

The children all nodded and Wilbur said

"That was where I won the competition last year for having the best teeth and the prize was to come to work in the Lighthouse."

They all went back to the middle of the village and caught the bus to Paradise Bay. On the way they passed fields of crops that looked rather like the wheat that grew near Helen and Dudley's house.

"Those are oats to make our porridge" said Wilbur's Father.

"And there are the cows which make the milk to put on the porridge" said Polly pointing out of the window at a herd of Jersey cows that were a lovely light brown colour with big eyes and long eyelashes.

In the distance towards the centre of the Island they could see a large, very long building beside a forest of tall trees.

"What is that?' asked Andrew

"That is the factory where the famous Wilbur furniture is made." said Wilbur's Father. "Over a hundred Wilburs work there every weekday. They cut the trees in the forest and take off all the branches and leaves and a big circular saw cuts them into planks of wood which go on to a tall pile. Wilburs are very strong and can throw the pieces of wood on to the pile or carry them into the factory. Other Wilburs then make beautiful chairs and tables that are varnished and polished. They make bookcases and wooden beds, wardrobes and cupboards. They sell some to the other Cola Islands and some to countries in the world in exchange for fish and fruit, meat and pasta, television and radios and extra large washing machines. I used to work there before I retired making bunk beds for the Tufty people."

"So a lot of the furniture we have seen on Muddle and Great Tufty has been made in the Wilbur Furniture Factory." asked Andrew.

"Yes, the best comes from here. It is our biggest business on Rumbletum Island." Father Wilbur replied.

The bus passed through the town of Holestone where there was a rock standing on the beach with a hole in the middle made by the sea. It looked like a wonky polo mint.

Soon they entered Paradise Bay and saw flags and decorations and signs hanging from the buildings and a band was playing near the bus stop in the centre of the town. This was going to be fun. Everyone headed towards the fields behind the town where there were rows of seats in a small stadium. The grass area in the middle was marked with white lines. A rugby goal post was in the centre. At 2pm the Wilbur in charge, wearing a red peaked cap blew his whistle and two teams of six Wilburs ran on to the field – one team wearing blue and white shirts and shorts, and the other yellow and white. The loudspeaker announced that this was the final of the Rumbletum Thumpball Competition between the Wandering Wilburs in blue and The Wilbur Whizzers Wearing yellow.

For 15 minutes they thumped a metre wide round ball from each side of the rugby posts above the bar until one missed or the ball hit the ground. It was very close with The Wilbur Whizzers winning 14 – 12 and being presented with an enormous silver cup.

Next were the races once around the track for Wilburs of different age groups. Some were very close finishes and others were won by a long way. One lady Wilbur broke the record in the 'Mothers with two or more children' race. Dudley had misunderstood who could enter this race and thought the mothers and all the children should be running.

Big bags of oats were brought out. There were different weights.

There were ten competitors and they had to throw each weight over the bar in the H of the rugby posts. The Wilbur who managed to throw over the heaviest bag was the winner. The last two left in the competition were Wilbur Dirty Washing and Wilbur Flowerpot. They both managed heavier bags than the other competitors, but couldn't throw over the next highest weight. So they shared the prize.

As each event finished the cheering and the rumbling of tummies was deafening. The last event of the afternoon was the 'Shiniest Teeth Challenge' and Lighthouse Wilbur was asked to be the judge because he was the winner last year. Wilbur chose a young girl called Wilbur Daffodil and gave her a voucher for free bus rides anywhere on the Island for a whole year.

The Games finished with a tug-of-war won by The Holestone Heavers for the second year running. Then there was dancing as the band played and dozens of Wilburs laughed and danced on the grass where the games had been played. Wilbur and Polly were the first to begin the dancing. Helen had spotted an Ice Cream Stand and ordered a '99'.

She spent the next ten minutes trying to eat the most enormous cone before it melted.

Andrew and Dudley found another stall with giant hot dogs, whilst Wilbur's Mother bought some flapjacks and had them wrapped up for Dudley to take home. Dudley remembered to thank Wilbur's Mum for his present and there were lots of cuddles to say 'goodbye' led by Polly.

Wilbur came on the bus back to the ferry with them and two of his friends came as well. They were Wilbur Doctor and Wilbur Wellington Boots.

"Hey Boots. Come and tell my friends about the day we all cycled around the whole island

when we were boys." called out Wilbur Lemonade.

Boots made it into a funny story telling
them that their Wilbur kept pretending to fall

off his bike and hurt himself. It was each time they passed an ice cream shop and he made them buy him an ice cream to make him better before he would ride on.

"It took us all day to go all the way round" said Wilbur Doctor "and Lemonade here had about six ice creams."

Wilbur Doctor then told them that he was working in the hospital as a male nurse and that his name now was Nurse Wilbur Doctor.

"It is very confusing for the patients. They sometimes think I am a doctor and ask questions that I can't answer. But soon it will be even more confusing in the hospital. One of the Wilburs training to be a doctor was born when his mother was talking to a nurse, so he is called Wilbur Nurse. When he finishes his training he will be Doctor Wilbur Nurse. So, in the hospital then, we shall have Doctor Wilbur Nurse and me, Nurse Wilbur Doctor."

"Ha, ha, ha. That is a problem" laughed Helen.

The bus came around the island road up to the jetty. The Wilburs asked the driver to stop and three Wilburs and four children stepped off and walked down the stone jetty. There was no sign of the ferry and it was nearly 6pm, the time Toby Tornado said he would be there. It was almost 7.30pm before they saw a ferry coming around the headland and heading for the jetty. When it arrived it was the ferry from Great Bear Island bringing lots of Wilburs home after a day's shopping in the big town on their other island.

The Trainee Superhero stepped onto the jetty wearing an electric blue cape over a short yellow dress with the letter T on the front.

"Hallo. I am Typhoon Tamsin. Are you in any trouble because I am very good at helping people who have a problem?" she asked.

"Do you know where Toby Tornado is?" asked Andrew. "He was due to collect us in a Wilbur Ferry at 6pm."

"I'll find out." she said and began to speak to her wrist as one of the superheroes had done before. "Toby sends his apologies. His ferry has broken down and needs attention to the engine. He has asked me to take you home as I have finished my work for the day. How many passengers do you have? Are all these Wilburs coming?"

"Only the four of us" said Andrew. "Our friends have come to see us safely to the jetty."

"Bye Wilburs. Thank you" More cuddles

from Polly and off they went with Typhoon Tamsin as the pilot/driver.

CHAPTER SEVENTEEN

A FRIGHTENING MEETING

The rest of that day was very tiring. They had set off in the rocket ferry in the morning, spent a whole day on Rumbletum Island and returned to find it was only one minute after they had left and still morning at the Lighthouse.

Jeremy Junglie suggested they went up to his rooms and slept for a few hours in the Junglie beds. Everybody slept for nearly three hours and then they were greeted with plates of delicious sliced fruit – peaches, pears, raspberries, kiwi fruit and mangoes.

The children thanked the Junglies and set off back up the river to the slipway. They cycled home and put their bikes in the garage.

"You must be hungry because you didn't come home for lunch" said Auntie Maggie.

"Our friends gave us lots of lovely fruit for lunch" said Polly.

"You mean a sort of picnic" said Mum

"Yes, a sort of picnic. They eat a lot of fruit and you are always telling us to eat five-a-day." said Helen.

"Good. I am glad to hear your friends eat the best food. Now, come and have tea. Wash your hands and sit at the table."

The next day was rainy and they had to stay

indoors talking and playing video games. The sky cleared later in the afternoon, but it was too late to think of more adventures outside.

Andrew and Helen watched some of the News on television and then the local Westcountry News on the programme 'Spotlight.'

"People on holiday are being asked not to feed the wild ponies on Dartmoor" said the Newsreader. "Buns, sandwiches and pasties are not good for them and some have had to be treated by a vet." "We have just heard that another Sports Shop has been burgled this evening. The owners had closed the shop early to go to a cricket match where the players were using their equipment and, when they came back, they found that boxes of football shirts and shorts had been stolen. The thieves broke in through the rear window in broad daylight. Police think it is the same gang that has already raided three other shops in Devon recently."

Helen said quietly "Andy. They must be the men who came to Puffin Island store room. What can we do?"

"They will probably bring the stolen goods to the store this evening.

I have a plan to stop them getting into the store."

"What good will that do?" asked Helen

"If they can't get into the store they will go back up the river with the stolen boxes. I can then call the Police on my mobile, who will come and catch them further up the river. Then nobody will come and search the Lighthouse and discover our friends."

"How will you stop them getting into the storeroom" Helen asked.

"Let's go. I'll tell you on the way"

Polly and Dudley came into the room at that moment.

"Where are you going?" Polly asked.

"To the Lighthouse."

"We are coming too."

"You had better stay here. We may be late home" said Andrew.

"We are coming. It's another adventure and I am not missing it" squealed Dudley.

"OK. But we must leave a note for Mum" said Helen, taking a piece of paper and pen and writing 'Gone to Mr. Kerslake's boathouse – back soon. Love Helen."

Andrew and Helen told the others what they had heard on the TV as they rode along and when they were in Huckleberry.

Once at Puffin Island they moored Huckleberry in the usual way, rang the code on the

'Grown-up alarm" – twice, twice and once. They all ran to the hatch, opened it, down the steps and along the passageway. At the top of the stairs to the inside door of the Lighthouse stood Turnip.

"You have come very late today" he said

"It's an emergency" said Helen and told him what they had heard on the News.

They all went together back to the stone store and Andrew lifted the stone and took out the key again. The little frog hopped away again. He was getting rather fed up with being disturbed. Andrew replaced the key with an old key of the same size that had been hanging in Uncle Ray's garage. He put the store key in his pocket.

"If they come, Turnip, they will find our boat on the beach. Can you ask the new Wilbur to open the sliding doors so that I can row around and hide it inside the cavern on the lake?"

"I will go back and get Wilbur Lampshade to open the doors. You get the boat" said Turnip.

"Helen, come with me. Dudley, Polly go down with Turnip." Andrew ran back to the beach. He and Helen rowed around the rocky island and in through the sliding doors to the lake. Wilbur closed the doors behind them.

Polly and Dudley were told to go up to Turnip's room and stay there. Andrew and Helen went to sit on a rock near the white stone storeroom. It was beginning to get dark.

They all waited for half-an-hour. It was quiet and calm without any wind. The stars began to come out and wink at them. Suddenly they heard a distant 'chugg, chugg' of an engine.

"It may be them, or it could be a fishing boat. Let's find a good hiding place to watch" said Andrew.

There was a tall rock about 20 metres from the store door and far enough away for them to watch and not be discovered. In the dim light they could see the motor boat heading for the island. It was not a fishing boat and must be the same one they had heard when they were returning with the winkle team.

The bell inside the Lighthouse rang to tell them that grown-ups were coming on to their island. Everyone hid.

"Where is Dudley?" asked Turnip

"I don't know" answered Polly "He was here just a minute ago."

Dudley had heard the bell and run back down the cavern stairs and along the passage-way. He was pushing with all his might to open the hatch so that he could climb out and see what was happening.

Helen peered around the rock and saw two people carrying a heavy box. She pulled her head back into hiding

"They are coming" she whispered to Andrew.

"Stay still and listen" said Andrew.

The men heaved the big cardboard box up to the front of the store. Then there was a scrabbling noise near Helen's rock as one of them found the hidden key. The man's feet shuffled along the gravel as he returned along the path towards the store.

There was a 'click click' sound.

"The key doesn't fit the lock."

"It must fit" said another voice "We were using it only a few days ago."

"I'll keep trying. You go back and get another box. Ask Arthur if he has brought the spare key"

Andrew thought 'I didn't expect them to have a spare key."

Arthur and the man who fetched him came along carrying another box.

"The boat is all right on the beach. I put out the anchor. Let me have a go. Are you sure you put the right key under the stone?"

"Of course I'm sure. There was only one key"

"I haven't brought the spare with me. Have we got another padlock if we break this one?"

"Only back at my house. We could leave the store unlocked and come back with another padlock later."

"One of the fishermen may come by and have a look inside. Better we take the boxes back and put them somewhere else safe."

Andrew thought 'This is going well. My plan is working. When they go I will call the Police on my phone and they will come down and catch them on the river.'

"I wonder if I could have dropped it along here" said one of the men as he walked further down the path towards the secret hatch. "Hey, hey you. Come here! Arthur, Jim, there's a boy here" he called as he ran after him.

"We'll go round the other side and catch him" said Arthur.

As Dudley ran round the Lighthouse he ran straight into the arms of one of the men coming the other way down the path.

"Take him back to the store where I left my torch" said Jim

Dudley was struggling but Arthur held on to him tightly.

Behind the rock, Helen whispered.

"What a fool Dudley is. Now we have been discovered."

"Just wait and see what happens before we show ourselves" said Andrew. He looked up and saw Turnip's face at his window.

The men dragged Dudley to the front of the store

"Why are you here on the Island?"

"I like it" said Dudley "I often come here"

"What! In the dark? And how did you get here – swim?"

"I am a good swimmer. I can swim about five miles." replied Dudley.

"Ha. Rubbish. No-one your age could swim five miles" said Jim

"Have you taken our key?"

Two of the men were holding Dudley. They were all facing the store except Arthur, who had the torch and was leaning against the store door shining it at Dudley. Suddenly he saw something behind them and his hand started shaking.

"Oh My God" he said "It's a …….. It's an enormous…….It's a giant wild………"

The other men looked behind them and one said

"What is? I can't see anything."

242

"Right behind Jim. Look. A great hairy monster. Watch out!"

"Don't be daft Arthur. There's nothing there."

Arthur moved away from the door and cried

"Run, run for the boat" he shouted. "Come on. Leave the boxes"

The two others looked at each other, one still holding Dudley. A large hairy hand picked up Jim by his jacket collar, and put him down again two metres further down the path.

"Aarrggh!" came a strangled noise from his throat as the front of his jacket pulled against his neck. "What on earth was that??"

The other man still held Dudley, but Jim was already running after Arthur.

The last man began to follow them, still dragging Dudley. He immediately let him go when a large hairy arm went around the man's waist and he was carried down the path towards the beach.

"Hey, hey, help, stop it. What's going on? Mind my head on the rock. Who is this? Help. Where are you taking me? You've got huge hairy arms. Arrgh...it's a Gorilla!!" He was carried all the way back to his boat under the hairy arm and thrown into the sea beside the motorboat with a splash!

Andrew and Helen came out from behind their rock and followed.

"Get away, go away. Watch out, he's coming on to the boat" said Arthur. Jim was on board and the third man was climbing up the side of the motor boat, dripping water. Before they could start the motor the boat began to go fast backwards off the beach and out through the rocks towards the sea.

"Something's pushing us" shouted the third man.

"Of course it is. Can't you see its great bear head and those huge white teeth that look like they could bite off your arm. It's pushing us."

The boat sped out backwards with Arthur desperately trying to start the engine and one man still clinging to the side.

Andrew was laughing and laughing, so much that he had to sit down.

Dudley joined him, looking rather glum and said nothing. Helen clapped her hands "Well done, Wilbur Lampshade, you have saved us all!"

A wet Wilbur smiled with his lovely white teeth and went up the slope to watch with the children.

Whilst they watched a blue light began

flashing near the mouth of the river and a fast police launch came towards them, quickly catching up with the crooks' boat. It stopped beside the other boat and the children heard a voice say

"It's our old friend Arthur Hopkins. I thought it may be you when one of the witnesses said she saw someone with blond hair and striking blue eyes. Come with us and we'll have a little chat about some sports equipment."

The two boats were only 30 or 40 metres away from the Island and in the quiet of the night the children heard

"There's a terrible monster on that island. It tried to kill us and eat us. It's a giant gorilla". "No. It's more like a grizzly bear." "You didn't feel it." "No, but I could see it." "No, you couldn't. It was invisible."

'Of course I could see it. Look, there it is again".

They all looked at the Island, but only Arthur, with his blue eyes, could see Wilbur waving to him. The children had gone to find Polly.

"Yes, yes Arthur" said a police voice "And I expect we could find crocodiles and elephants and even a Superhero as well, ha ha ha."

The police launch went away up the river

with three crooks in handcuffs and a constable followed them in the motor boat.

CHAPTER EIGHTEEN

TIME TO GO HOME

Turnip and Polly and all seven Junglies came out to join them and they went back to stand on the rocks watching the blue light on the police launch disappearing around the distant bend in the river.

"What an adventure!" said Polly, who had been watching it all from Turnip's window "Dudley nearly spoilt it, but Wilbur Lampshade saved us all."

Turnip and Jeremy Junglie explained that they were going to have a busy night packing all their belongings. They had to leave the Lighthouse now, at least for a while, because the Police would come back to collect all the stolen goods, and will probably want to search the Lighthouse in case the crooks had hidden anything inside.

They had contacted the Cola Council, who had told them to leave the Lighthouse or they may be discovered. They were sending three ferries tomorrow in the early morning. One will be a Bank Ferry to collect all the winkle money and two will be for all the Junglies and Tufties and Flummocks and their belongings. This Wilbur will stay and move his CDs and things down into the secret room in the cavern where the sailing boat is stored.

"No-one will ever find the opening to his room, even if they found the cavern." said

Jeremy "And he will signal us when it is safe to come back again to collect more money."

"So, by tomorrow morning we will have gone." said Turnip.

"We will be able to see you again, won't we" said Polly with a tear in her eye.

"Oh Yes. Many times in the future. During your school holidays and when we come to collect more money for our Banks. Please come to see Wilbur to keep him company and give him some eggs for his tea."

There were lots of hugs and goodbyes. Tania, Tilly and Tufties joined in and even Freddie Flummock, although he didn't seem to know what was happening. They all returned to the cavern and the children jumped into Huckle-berry, who was waiting patiently on the cavern lake before being rowed out through the big doors and around the island to the river.

Polly and Dudley hoisted the sail, which helped them move up the river to the slipway. The moon had risen and the stars were watch-ing them, and a few ducks and waterbirds squawked as they went by at the end of yet another adventure on this holiday. There were only two holiday days left before Polly and Andrew would be collected by their Dad, and they and Auntie Maggie would drive away until they returned at Christmas.

When the children reached the house there was a 'welcome party' of one Dad and two Mums, all looking concerned and anxious.

"Where have you all been at this time of the night?" asked Dad

They all looked at the clock on the kitchen wall. It was 10.30pm. Later than any of them had realized.

"We were worried because you are too young to be running around after dark."

None of them knew quite how much to tell without talking about their friends.

"Well, Mr. Kerslake called us to say you were all safe and cycling home. How did he know you were out tonight?"

"I don't know" said Helen "He must have seen us come back in our boat when we pulled it up his slipway."

"A policeman is coming to talk to you tomorrow morning. What is he coming to talk about?"

The children all began to talk at the same time. They realized that their Cola Islands friends would have gone tomorrow, so they shared the adventures with their parents. It was too late for them to be discovered.

"Stop!" said Dad "One at a time please, and begin at the beginning."

They told about the Lighthouse and the cavern lake and misty days and sliding doors, about the express lift and the delicious food. And then all about Tufties and Flummocks and Junglies and a huge Wilbur, the Superheroes and rocket ships, about swinging in the Junglie trees, cola waterfalls and Wilbur games, muddled Flummocks and lots of eggs.

"So that is why you needed all those eggs" interrupted Auntie Maggie

"We thought there was something strange about the eggs."

Then they told about the winkle shell money and how there had been men coming at night to put boxes in the store room with the padlock. They had read about the burglaries in Dad's paper and then had seen the News tonight about the latest break-in. The men were likely to bring the things they had stolen to the same place as the others.

Andrew finished the story with his decision to change the key so that the men would take the boxes back. He would then call the Police who would catch the crooks. It all went wrong but, with Wilbur's help, the Police came anyway and caught the gang.

"We only went out late because we wanted to get the gang caught and put in prison." said Dudley.

"How did the Police know where to come if you didn't actually phone them?" asked Dad.

"It's a mystery. They must have been following them all the time." answered Andrew.

There were other mysteries too. How did the Police know which house to call on even if perhaps the crooks had told them that Dudley was also on the Island? How did the Police think that one small boy had chased three men off the Island and frightened them too? Why did the children need so much sleep on their holiday? Why was Polly wearing a badge on her T shirt that said 'Be a Friend to a Flummock'?

"This is all very strange" said Dad "But I expect we will hear more from the policeman in the morning."

The children went to bed but, this time, they couldn't sleep very well.

They were thinking of how Wilbur Lampshade had been so brave and sadly that it may be a long time before they saw all their Cola friends again.

*

Andrew was pleased to see that it was misty in the morning because it would mean that the three ferries could come into the cavern lake, and take all the money, luggage and everyone to the Cola Islands. He was also sad that they had to stay in the house instead of racing to catch a rocket ferry waiting under the Lighthouse.

The policeman arrived at 10am and was wearing his uniform and he had a trim beard and glasses as well. He brought a policewoman with him, who was pretty and friendly to all the children. Dad had stayed away from work to find out what had happened. He and the two Mums made up nine people in the sitting room, some sitting on easy chairs and some on dining chairs.

"We have come to find out what happened on Puffin Island last night and to thank you for helping us to catch a gang of thieves who have taken goods that don't belong to them."

"Tennis Rackets." said Dudley, who thought it was about time he said something.

"How did you know about the tennis rackets?" asked the lady.

"We saw them in a big box in the store." said Polly

"Do you mean there were more boxes inside the store on the Island?

If so, how did you get in, because we couldn't this morning? We have sent away for a metal cutter to cut off the padlock, which has not yet arrived."

Andrew handed her the key.

"I hid it so that they couldn't get back inside."

"That was clever. It probably means that all the stolen goods from three or four shops are inside the storeroom" said the policeman.

"How did you manage to frighten them so much that they are all refusing to come back with us to open the store?"

"We had some help from a friend." said Andrew quickly.

"He must have been a very strong friend."

"He is" said Polly "Strong, but very cuddly."

"May we talk to him?"

"We think he has gone away and he is very shy talking to grown-ups" added Helen.

"Are you going to search the Lighthouse as well?" asked Dad

"Yes Sir. We are. That also has a big padlock, so we need a cutter for that too.

"May I come with you if you do? I am concerned about my children being able to get in there and want to see if it is safe." added Dad

"Yes Sir. If you wish. Come with us now. We are going across again in the police launch. Goodbye children. Remember though. If you see or hear anything like this again, phone us before you do anything else.

You know our number."

"999" said Dudley, who was good at numbers.

After they had gone Helen was taking her trainers out of the washing machine again and she overheard Mum saying to Aunt Maggie

"Ray doesn't believe any of that rubbish about Wilburs and Junglies. He thinks the children have made it all up and are having a 'pretend' adventure holiday"

"Well, it does seem quite fantastic" said Aunt Maggie "I was believing it until they mentioned Superheroes and Cola Waterfalls. Lets see if Ray finds a three-metre tall Teddy Bear in the Lighthouse ha,ha,ha"

Helen told the others what she had heard. Polly told her that she had already told Dudley that no-one at school would believe him.

'WE KNOW it is true and that is all that matters.' Polly thought. 'Even if Wilbur was there, Uncle Ray would not be able to see him because he has brown eyes.'

The rest of the day went slowly. Andrew decided that they should not try to reach the Island again because there would be policemen and Helen's Dad there, all looking for stolen goods and Tufties and Wilburs.

The Police found all they needed to put the three men away for a long time. There were two boxes of hockey sticks left on the men's boat that they had taken away last night, and two more boxes of football boots and shirts sitting outside the storeroom. With Andrew's key they unlocked the padlock and discovered eight more boxes inside including Dudley's tennis rackets and some papers that one of the men had left behind, showing that he had been there before.

Helen and Dudley's Dad however, did not expect to find any evidence of Wilburs , Junglies or Tufties. And he didn't. Everything had gone except for a Wilbur hiding in the rocky boathouse below. He did find the cover of one of his wife's CDs in the glass room where the Lighthouse light used to be, and this was rather puzzling. There was also a funny squidgy thing on the top of the building that had all the air taken out of it – like a deflated bouncy castle. Below it was a lift shaft that he assumed the lighthouse men had once used to move heavy equipment up from the base, with a stop at each of the three rooms. He went into these, but there was nothing to be seen in any of them.

The Police put a new padlock on the Lighthouse main door. Nobody discovered the other entrance that came through a cupboard from the cavern, so they found nothing about the lake or the cavern, or a hiding Wilbur Lampshade.

That evening at dinnertime Dad said

"You all have a wonderful imagination if you think we believe all this nonsense about Junglie Tree Houses and Giant Wilbur buses. There was nothing in the Lighthouse except a lot of old junk left behind by the Lighthouse men when they stopped needing the Light. The only thing I found was this CD cover – the same as one of the CDs that Mum has."

Mum did not say anything but thought it was odd that the old Lighthouse men had listened to the same music as she did. She made a mental note to ask Helen who had borrowed her copy of this CD. She thought there was no way this cover could be hers because Helen could not have got into the Lighthouse.

Quietly the children went upstairs to their rooms. They met in Helen's bedroom and there was a lot of whispering and talking in low voices before they noticed that Polly had fallen asleep and thought they should too.

CHAPTER NINETEEN

SUPERCOLA

The last day of their summer holiday in Devon with their cousins was a misty morning. Polly and Andrew were first downstairs to gobble down their breakfast and to encourage Dudley and Helen to waste no time setting off down the familiar stream path. They came to the narrow bridge across the stream that only had room for one bike at a time. Polly and Dudley tried to enter the bridge together. Polly was first and Dudley hit the post of the handrail and fell into the water with a huge yell and a splash. The other three laughed and laughed as poor Dudley crawled up the grassy bank with water pouring out of his hair and clothes and shoes.

As he walked his trainers went 'squelch' and

a fountain of water came out of the side of each one.

"Ugh" he said "I think I had a mouthful of river weed and even a few tadpoles."

"You can't come to the Island like that" said Andrew "Go back and change your clothes. Take my bike whilst I mend your bent mudguard and dry your brakes."

Dudley came back ten minutes later wearing a new set of clothes

"Mum wasn't very pleased and Aunt asked me if I had managed to catch any fish for lunch."

On they went, past where the ladies had fallen into the hedge and come out covered in thorns and prickles, to Mr. Kerslake's boathouse. He was in there this time, binding the end of a piece of rope.

"Hallo. Off to your island again? You have had an exciting two weeks haven't you?"

"Yes" said Polly "the best adventures ever."

"Would you all like to come to the house for tea this afternoon before you have to break up 'The Fantastic Four'?" he asked.

"Are we 'The Fantastic Four'?" asked Dudley excitedly.

"That is what I call you." Mr. Kerslake replied. "You can row, you can sail, you cycle, you fly in rockets, you swing in trees and you catch burglars. That is all pretty fantastic."

"Yes please" said Andrew "We would love to come. What time is the best for you?"

"Come at 4 o'clock. There is someone I want you to meet."

They went over to Huckleberry and launched him into the river, pulled up the sail, and swept off down the river to their Island of adventure. The mist was not too thick and was swirling like it had been when they went to Rumbletum.

"There is no hurry" said Helen "We shall not be flying on any ferries today. That is finished for a while."

They walked slowly to the hatchway without ringing the 'Grown-up alarm' because there was no-one in the Lighthouse to hear it. Down they went into the cavern and they noticed that the pink light was on giving the cavern and the lake a friendly glow. Watching the screen that was beside the lever that controlled the sliding doors was Wilbur, with his suitcase on the ground next to him.

"Hallo Wilbur, are you all right here on your own?" asked Polly.

"Halloo everyone" his growly voice said back, accompanied by a loud tummy rumble.

"Why do you have your bag packed" Helen asked.

"I am waiting for the Wilbur Ferry to bring back Wilbur Lemonade, and then I go home." Polly ran over and gave him a hug.

"You have been a brave and clever Wilbur and you helped catch all those nasty men" she said.

"Yes. But now I have to go back to my real job on the Ostrich Farm whilst Lemonade comes back to his job here."

"We'll miss you, Wilbur" said Helen and the others nodded, especially Dudley, who had been rescued by him.

"The ferry is coming now" he said and moved towards the lever to open the sliding rock doors. In came the special Wilbur Ferry and moored at the platform inside the cavern. Out came Wilbur Lemonade to be greeted by Polly. A very official-looking Junglie wearing a peaked cap, a silver shirt and long shorts followed

"I am glad you are all here" said the smart Junglie. "I am the official representative of the Cola Council and I have come to invite you to attend a special medal ceremony on Supercola Island. Can you come now?"

"Yes we can" answered Andrew "But what is this all about?"

"You will see and be pleased when you arrive there." the official Junglie replied.

They all climbed into the ferry and greeted Toby Tornado, who was still sitting in the pilot seat adjusting one of the dials. He stood up and returned the greeting by banging his fist on his chest in salute.

"I apologise for the breakdown when you

were waiting for me on Rumbletum. I have been having a few problems with this Wilbur Ferry."

He said in his deep, manly voice. They sat in the giant seats again and the official Junglie looked very small in his seat with his seatbelt wrapped around him twice.

Toby motored out of the cavern and they left their favourite Wilbur to close the doors. The rocket ferry zoomed off towards Supercola Island, the capital of all the Cola Islands, and where the Council made all the important decisions that affected all the Cola people everywhere. They landed close to a beautiful harbour with grand buildings behind it. They could see Carrot Cars driving around in the same way as on Great Tufty.

Toby Tornado moved up to the dock and moored amongst several other ferries and small luxury boats. The official Junglie was met by a Carrot Car with two extra sections and seats for all five people. They said 'goodbye' to Wilbur with a Polly hug and Toby said he would go on to Rumbletum Island to take Wilbur home.

The driver of the car saluted the children and climbed into the driver's seat and they drove along to a building that looked like a small castle with flags flying from masts outside. They were taken inside to a large reception room and greeted by a line of older Cola Islanders, all looking very smart or in uniforms wearing hats. The children were asked to sit in four seats at the front. Behind them was a row of Cola Folk dressed in their best clothes.

When everybody had sat down an elderly Tufty stood up and welcomed all the visitors

"This special occasion is the annual Festival of Superheroes Special Awards when we present medals to the people the Superheroes have nominated for being the kindest and most helpful to others during the year. First I would like to thank the Training Superheroes for their list of medal winners. Everyone clapped and looked to one side where they could see a line of all the Trainee Superheroes, some of whom the children had met on the ferries.

They looked at the ones they knew, all dressed in their colorful outfits, with sunglasses, helmets, and headbands. They all seemed to wear their shorts outside their bodysuits. All the bright colours of the rainbow were there in their outfits. Superhealer Sheila, with her gold star headband, was next to Typhoon Tamsin. Toby Tornado was standing beside the first

Hero they met – Zebedee Zoom. Wonderful Winston, wearing new boots with little wings on them, Rupert Rocket and five others they had not seen before. Zebedee waved to them when he saw them looking.

Medals, with ribbons attached, were put around the necks of each of the Cola people to get special awards. The President Tufty shook their hands and put the ribbons over each head so that the shiny medals would hang on their chests. Then he said

"Several of the Trainee Superheroes have asked me to present special medals to four friends from England, who have been kind to many Cola people in the last weeks. They have helped collect money from the rocks for our Banks and brought eggs for gifts for our workers living in the Lighthouse. They have been 'Friends to Flummocks" and are loved by people all over the Cola Islands. Only two days ago they helped to catch thieves who were coming to the Lighthouse Island and could have seen our folk when they were working.

Therefore it gives me great pleasure to present a Gold Medal to Andrew, - and to Helen – and Godfrey, sorry I mean Dudley – and a special Gold Medal with fur around it to Polly, because of her extra love for Wilburs"

The children stood up and went to collect their medals. Everyone in the room clapped and cheered as they walked past the line of Trainee Superheroes, who all banged their fists on their chests at the same time in salute.

The President then said

"Finally, I am very pleased to tell you all that Wonderful Winston has been made a Full Superhero! He has passed all his tests with flying colours" He presented Wonderful Winston with a new bodysuit, which had his name on it in silver letters, to wear instead of the one with the big capital T on the front. The President shook Winston's hand and Winston saluted to a deafening round of applause.

After the ceremony the children were taken to a smaller room with tables and chairs and given a glass of butterscotch cola each, a giant cherry flapjack and a melt-in-your-mouth scone with cream and jam.

Lots of the people on Supercola were waiting along the route back to the harbour to cheer the children and the Cola Councillor, who drove by in the new pink Carrot Car made this year on Tiny Tufty. They drove by a large building marked 'Cola Bank' and the Councillor explained that all the new money from the Lighthouse collectors had been taken there for counting before some was sent out to each island for people to use.

More people waved and cheered as they pulled up beside a different passenger ferry, next to which was waiting new Superhero Wonderful Winston in his new bodysuit and the white boots with little wings attached. He said in his deep, manly voice

"I asked the President to let me fly you back to your Lighthouse. My first job as a Full Superhero."

"Thank you" said Dudley thinking that this will be one Superhero he has met that his school friends will soon see in a film or on TV.

When they sat behind him in the rocket ferry and everything around it was a blur, Helen asked Winston what kind of wonderful work he was planning to do in the world.

"I have very strong hands" he replied. "And with my finger I can drill into the earth quickly and a long way down. Many people do not have enough water to drink or wash with. I shall go to their countries and find out where the water is underground. Then I shall push my finger into the earth and dig a well all the way down to the water supply and fix a pump at the top. I will then leave it for the people in the nearest villages to collect and drink whenever they are thirsty, or wash whenever they are feeling dirty."

"You will be very popular and a true Superhero" said Andrew as he watched the sliding doors open and saw their Wilbur waiting on the rock platform beside the lake. They shook hands with Wonderful Winston and said they would look out for him on TV. He saluted and said 'goodbye' in an even deeper manly voice than usual because he was now a Full Superhero.

Polly welcomed Wilbur Lemonade with a cuddle and showed him her special furry Wilbur Gold Medal. He closed the big doors behind Winston as he left with the ferry in the mist. Wilbur went with them to the hatchway and Helen promised to bring him eggs and some other food next weekend. The children walked back across the rock surface and along the path to Huckleberry, who was patiently waiting on the beach, half in the water and half on the sand.

"I feel sad" said Helen "We are at the end of so many lovely adventures."

"It is still only 10.30am" said Andrew, his medal swinging against his T shirt. "Let's take Huckleberry home this time. We can walk to Mr. Kerslake's house this afternoon when we go to tea with him, and ride our bikes home."

The wind was getting stronger and blowing down the river so they couldn't use the sail to help. Helen and Andrew rowed hard and turned left in to the entrance of the stream. Dudley was looking over the bow and could see several trout in the clear water ahead.

"I can see lots of fish. They are quite big" he said.

"I shall come fishing with you next time I come to stay" said Andrew "We can catch our dinner of tasty brown trout."

Stupid was waiting for them as they walked

into the garden probably hoping that they had caught a fish for him. Andrew used the stream water to wash down the outside of Huckleberry before securing him to the post at the bottom of the garden. They neatly stacked the oars inside the boat and packed the sail and ropes in the canvas bag.

After lunch they sat with their feet dangling in the cool stream for the last time and went through their adventures one by one. Dudley said

"I was with you this year for every one of them."

They had not told him about the nighttime expedition with the Winkle Team.

During lunch Aunt Maggie and Mum wanted to know what the large medals were for. All four had them hanging on the ribbons around their necks.

"They are a special award from the Cola Islands President for being nice to everyone." said Polly.

"I suppose this will be another of your stories about Wilburs and Tufties" said Aunt "Don't go telling these tales to your friends. They will think your have gone mad. We don't believe you and Uncle Ray doesn't believe a word of it."

"But, it is all true!" said Dudley

"Yes, dear, and I am a monkey's uncle" said Mum.

"That's silly" said Helen "Anyway you would be the monkey's auntie if you were."

They went upstairs to change in to smarter clothes and left the house at 3.15pm to walk to Mr. Kerslake's for tea.

"No-one will ever believe our stories" said Polly.

CHAPTER TWENTY

THE BIGGEST SURPRISE OF ALL

They knocked on the front door of Mr. Kerslake's big white house.

He answered the door and invited them inside.

"Wipe your shoes on the mat." Helen said to Dudley.

"My wife has gone shopping. But come into the sitting room and meet a good friend of mine" said Mr. Kerslake.

They went into a large sitting room and there, sitting on the sofa, because it was the only seat big enough for him, was THEIR WILBUR.

"Wilbur!" screeched Polly "Wilbur, why are you here?" she said, running across the room to cuddle next to him on the sofa

"He has come to join us for tea" said Mr.

Kerslake as he followed them into the room.

"You KNOW our Wilbur?" exclaimed Helen in amazement.

"Yes. I know him very well indeed. In fact I have just fetched him from Puffin Island in my cabin cruiser.

Andrew was looking thoughtful.

"When we saw you this morning you said we were your 'Fantastic Four'. One of the reasons you said was that we swing in trees. The only place we have been swinging in trees has been on Bungle Jungle in the Cola Islands. Did Wilbur tell you we had been there?"

"Yes. You have worked it out correctly. Wilbur and I talk quite often about all sorts of things. He told me how you have been having adventures on the other islands during the last two weeks.

"Did he tell you how we caught the burglars," asked Dudley.

"No. I knew about that because I became involved myself. You see, I have been watching everything that has been happening on Puffin Island for a long time. Go over to the window and take a look through my telescope."

The children saw a big telescope on a tripod in the bay window of Mr. Kerslake's wide room and Dudley and Andrew went to look through it.

The telescope was pointing at the Lighthouse and Dudley could clearly see into the glass room at the top of the building. Andrew then had a go and turned it towards the store, where he could see clearly the door with its new padlock.

"This is a lovely telescope and you can see very clearly for a long way." he said.

"Well, Wilbur and I have a system of signals. He has a box of numbers and each number from 1 to 9 means something different.

They tell me what is happening on the Island. If he holds up No.1 it means 'Everything is fine and everyone is happy.' No.2 means 'The Winkle Team are out tonight'. No.3 means 'A new visitor has come to the Island.'

"What is No.7?" asked Polly

"No.7 means 'Polly is cuddling me again'.

Everyone laughed.

"I have been watching the men bringing boxes to that stone store room. The telescope has an 'infra-red' lens which enables me to see through it in the dark. I guessed they were storing something illegal or they would have come in daylight."

"We found their key and went inside to see what was in the boxes" said Helen.

"I saw you go inside, but I didn't know what they had in there and I didn't know your plan to hide the key. I thought it would be a good idea for the Police to check and, when their motor boat went by that last evening, I was in my boathouse. I ran back here and phoned the Police for them to come in the police launch that they keep further up the river."

"I was going to phone them too, so that the men would be caught with the stolen goods still on their boat. I thought they would take them back up the river when they found the door key was missing and they couldn't get in." added Andrew.

"Your plan would have worked if they hadn't caught Dudley. It made me laugh a lot when I saw the other Wilbur carrying one of the crooks and throwing him in the sea. I didn't know what they were stealing but the Fantastic Four had worked out that it was linked with the break-ins at sports shops."

Mr. Kerslake left the room and spoke to someone else. Soon a lady came in pushing a trolley piled high with cakes and drinks, plates and knives.

"How many plates shall I leave?" she asked and counted the people in the room. "Five. I thought you said six, Mr.K" she said, leaving the room.

Dudley, who was good at maths, counted six in the room.

"There are six people. We need six plates." he said.

Mr. Kerslake and Andrew laughed and Mr. K explained

"What colour are my eyes, Dudley?"

"Sort of blue" said Dudley

"And what colour were Mrs Field's eyes?"

"I don't know."

"They were green" said Mr. Kerslake

'Of course' everyone thought 'She couldn't see Wilbur!"

They all enjoyed a delicious tea and then told about all the amazing food they had eaten, and drinks they had been given on their visits to the Cola Islands.

Mr. Kerslake said "I want to visit them too, one day. I will have to get permission from the Supercola Council to go. You see, my telescope can't see through the mist and the fog, so I haven't yet seen any of the superheroes or flown in a rocket ferry. However I am paid by the British Government to take care of the Cola Islanders who come here, and to keep their secret. Will you all keep their secret too?"

"Does that mean we can't tell anyone at school?" asked Dudley, looking upset.

"Not if you want them to come back to the Lighthouse." Mr. K replied. "You are the clever 'Fantastic Four'. Can you keep a fantastic secret?"

The four looked at each other, and then at Wilbur, and realised that if they did keep the secret they would be able to see him much more, perhaps every school holiday. They nodded to each other until Helen said

"Yes Mr. Kerslake, we can keep the secret."

Polly added "We have told my Mum and Aunt and Uncle and they say they don't believe a word of it. Probably no-one else would ever believe us anyway."

Mr. Kerslake said "Well. I know it's true and you can come here and talk about your Cola Friends whenever you like."

THE END

Acknowledgements

I am grateful to Seda Pheby for reading the early manuscript and advising me from her experience as a Primary School teacher.

Although retired for several years Rosemary Young has contributed all the drawings to stimulate our imagination. It is good to see she has lost none of her skills as a former Disney Illustrator.

Many thanks to her and to Jane Dixon-Smith for another stunning design for the cover of one of my books.

About the Author

Stuart Neil lives in East Devon. He played tennis at Junior Wimbledon and was a Scotland Hockey International. For many years he has led Emergency Medical Teams for European Charities working in crisis zones in Asia and Africa.

He has finally given in to the temptation to write and the novella 'The Tennis Racket' leads into his 'Erik Trilogy':-

'Second String to a Tennis Racket.'
'The Marbella String Quartet.'
'The Court Jester'

Three romantic ventures into the world of Tennis and Ladies Golf.

Each of these books or the 'Erik Box Set' may be purchased through the Amazon website.

The proceeds from all these books will be donated to Stuart's two charities:-

Star Action (Reg. Charity No. 1111137)
www.staraction.org

The Quiet Mind Centre (Reg. Charity No. 1029636)
www.quiet-mind.org

Printed in Great Britain
by Amazon